COUP D'ETAT

To:
my friend
Rod & Jane his
lovely wife,
my reluctant Manhattan
Buddy Rod.
Good Luck
Jim Harris

Coup D'etat

The Assassination of a President! What If
He Lived?

James J. Shanni

iUniverse, Inc.
New York Lincoln Shanghai

Coup D'etat
The Assassination of a President! What If He Lived?

iUniverse books may be ordered through booksellers or by contacting:

iUniverse
2021 Pine Lake Road, Suite 100
Lincoln, NE 68512
www.iuniverse.com
1-800-Authors (1-800-288-4677)

This is a work of historical fiction. Apart from the well known actual people, events, and locales that figure in the narrative, all names, characters, places and incidents are the products of the authors' imagination or are used fictitiously. Any resemblance to current events or locals or to living persons is entirely coincidental.

ISBN-13: 978-0-595-35541-9 (pbk)
ISBN-13: 978-0-595-67231-8 (cloth)
ISBN-13: 978-0-595-80026-1 (ebk)
ISBN-10: 0-595-35541-2 (pbk)
ISBN-10: 0-595-67231-0 (cloth)
ISBN-10: 0-595-80026-2 (ebk)

Printed in the United States of America

This book is dedicated to my lifelong soul mate, Evelyn, my wife of nearly forty-two years. We have made a lifelong journey together. When I was sixteen, Evelyn fifteen, we would often walk home from high school holding hands. I attended St. Mary's High School in downtown Jersey City she went to Dickinson High. I'd walk the two plus miles to meet her and then we'd walk two miles to her home. Our relationship has been filled with love from the very beginning. I thank her for her patience in putting up with my faults, no small number are they. Our joy in the early years was loving each other and having our three children. In later life it has been our grandchildren. With five boys, four of them three years old or less, a one-month-old granddaughter and one more on the way, we have truly been blessed, seven grandchildren, who would have thought. I honestly don't think it gets any better.

I would also like to make special mention of my friend John Evan. For years I would bounce ideas off John about this book and another I am currently working on. John was a good listener and would jokingly suggest, whenever the subject matter drifted from its original course, that he would have me writing yet another book. It got to the point that we would laugh heartily and frequently about the number of books he had me writing. John passed away in August 2004. One never really gets over the loss of a close friend or relative. John was a good friend who is and will always be sorely missed.

Foreword

Sometimes in the course of living life, we get caught up in just trying to make it through the day. Health problems, problems with finances, friction with loved ones or co-workers—for most of us, life presents many challenges. We all have obligations to ourselves to work hard to fulfill our desires and improve our position in life. We have obligations to our families, to ensure their emotional and physical well-being, to provide for their education, and to generally see to it that they grow up with a head start in life. This is the American way.

Sometimes it takes all our strength and most of our time to keep up with these goals. We have precious little discretionary time for doing some of the things *we* like to do. We tend to be less interested in things that don't seem to affect our everyday lives. Politics, for example, is a cutthroat, dirty business most of us shy away from.

According to voting records in many districts, only about 33 percent of Americans bother to vote. Many people are frustrated with political rhetoric and don't believe they can change anything. The close election of 2000 seems to have changed some of that. Politicians are just going to do whatever they want to anyway, we reason. Balance the budget, run the country's Defense system more efficiently, reduce the overall size of government so regular Americans can keep more of their hard-earned money—not a chance, they reason. Hundreds of millions of dollars in pork-barrel legislation, eight-hundred-dollar toilet seats, what's the use?

A little more than midway through the last century, Americans narrowly elected as president a person who was intent on doing what he promised. He was intent upon making a difference. Not everyone agreed with all of his positions on various political matters. To be sure he was no saint, but he was basically an honest man in politics to help make the country better. He was a wealthy man, worth millions, who grew up in a family worth hundreds of millions of dollars. He was used to having everything money could buy. Yet he was uncomfortable with fancy cars, and except for his simple wedding band, he wore no jewelry. From the time he was elected to Congress in 1947 until the day he was shot dead, he donated his salary to charity. He was immensely intelligent, reading twelve hundred words a minute, and he consumed written material faster than almost anyone. He went to the finest schools, and surrounded himself with both intellectuals and streetwise assistants.

At the time of his election, the United States was still paying for and carrying a military far too large for the times. Much of the military spending was to staff large headquarters staffs. In short, the U.S. military was too large and cumbersome and with the early onset of new technology, the U.S. government was spending far too much on obsolete weapons the country no longer needed. The president ordered a 15 percent cut in headquarters staff and was intent upon further review. For nearly ten years the United States had been lending military "assistance" to a country in the midst of a civil war halfway around the world. With military and defense contractors, hungry for major increases in defense appropriations, and anxious to substantially increase that assistance.

Instead he ordered huge reductions in our military personnel. He ordered large cutbacks into the U.S. commitment to defend Europe. He began to scale back the country's involvement in the assistance it was providing to an Asian country in the midst of war between democracy and communism. So to stop the military and CIA from continuing their clandestine defiance against his wishes, he ordered all military and the Iintelligence community, who were "in bed" with the military, as well as civilian CIA personnel, to clear all travel to that country with his office.

The president believed the United States should negotiate political solutions to problems that the admirals and generals wanted to resolve with military force. In his first 3 years in office, he had a number of serious disagreements with the Joint Chiefs of Staff. They were openly rebellious over the president's reductions in military personnel and budgets, so rebellious in fact, that several generals in acts heretofore unheard of, had hostile verbal exchanges during meetings with the President. They even openly threatened him.

Powerful people inside and outside the U.S. government conspired to kill the president and install someone who would do their bidding regarding the war and in general their status quo on the military. Their plot was months in the planning. It culminated when they seized upon their opportunity and assassinated the president. The American people were tremendously saddened to see their young, vigorous leader murdered in his prime. They mourned, there was a fitting military funeral, covered by news and television people, and it was over. We named a few streets and buildings after him then resumed our business of trying to take care of our families, ignoring with disdain politics and politicians.

Government officials immediately proclaimed the lone assassin responsible for killing the president had been captured. They covered up vital detail about the assassination. Compelling evidence that would have been strong enough to convict nearly anyone in Court. Evidence that would have caused any reasonable man to question how one man could have killed the president. Evidence, that covered up the true events of that day. The alleged lone gunman, who claimed he was innocent and that he had been set up as a patsy, was in custody less than three hours after the assassination and was murdered less than forty-eight hours later in front of TV cameras, silencing him forever. Although he was questioned by seasoned lawyers and CIA officers, he was never afforded his right to an attorney. These people were seasoned lawyers, they knew that as long as the accused assassin didn't have a lawyer present, whatever information they obtained during their questioning of this suspect without his attorney present would be inadmissible in court evidence. But they continued to question him, as if they knew that there would never be a trial.

These events could not have happened if Americans had truly cared about their country. The wrinkles in our belly are gone Americans have become overweight and greedy. There has never been an outcry for the truth in this matter, even though a poll shows 66 percent of Americans do not believe the official government story about the assassination. To this day, the truth has never come out. The truth will never come out as long as the American people don't care enough to have a real investigation into the murder of the president.

Are secrets about the assassination being withheld from the public in order to protect high-ranking government officials who played a part in the conspiracy? Photographs, evidence and first hand affidavits have been doctored beyond recognition in this case. The only official investigation was led by a panel of government insiders who labeled it top secret and conducted every interview in closed session. This book is a work of fiction, but it is based upon many of the actual facts surrounding the assassination. Something has changed in the United States in the last forty or fifty years. Elected officials have seized the country Americans founded for the people and by the people. The United States was formed as a republic, not a democracy. The differences are profound and should be studied by all discerning citizens.

The 2000 and 2004 U.S. elections should serve as a wake-up call for all Americans, regardless of which party they voted for. The United States has entered an era in which small, influential groups can dictate the outcome of elections. They can do so because the general public does not vote. Small groups elect senators and congressmen who then pass legislation that solidifies their positions. This will only end when large numbers of Americans take the time to inform themselves about the various issues and vote. Countries with far less than ours have been given the opportunity to vote and have turned out in numbers that double and triple our voter turnout. May God Bless America!!

CHAPTER 1

▼

WRONG PLACE, WRONG TIME

After working nearly five weeks with only two days off, Mike Reardon, full of anticipation and anxious to catch a few largemouth bass was on his way out of town eager to get to the small log cabin he had rented for three days. The cabin was about one and a half hours southeast of Dallas, on a five-hundred-acre lake surrounded by a forest of southern pine trees. Mike had rented a cabin on this lake several times before and was familiar with the landscape. He enjoyed the quiet and serenity of the surrounding woods while fishing he could almost smell the fresh scent of pine that permeated the air around the lake, especially in the early morning when the trees were dampened with the morning dew. The weather was unusually warm and sunny for this time of year. Late November usually marked the beginning of colder temperatures, but the forecast was promising at least three more days of balmy weather. Mike hadn't been fishing for months, and he was looking forward to the quiet time he would spend casting his line into the water. He needed to make one more stop to pick up an adequate supply of beer and some food for his three-day stay.

The trucking company where Mike worked as a senior rate clerk had been deluged all summer with freight coming in to Dallas for the Christmas holiday; he was ready and long overdue for this long weekend. The late summer and fall was one of the busiest periods of the year as companies stocked up for the Christmas season. In fact the period from around Labor Day in early September to the middle of November usually meant he had to work overtime three or four days a week just to keep up with rating and classifying the various types of freight. His job was tedious but very important as the classification given to the different kinds of freight would weigh heavily on the rate the truckers would charge for their freight-hauling services.

Mike was thirty-nine years old, a confirmed bachelor. He had grown up in Providence, Rhode Island, but as far as he knew had no family there or anywhere else. His parents had divorced when he was thirteen. It was a terribly insecure time for him. He had stayed with his mother, but not seeing his father every day left him feeling empty. He looked forward every year to the few weeks he would spend with his dad during the summer. He loved every minute of it, going on hunting and fishing trips, tinkering with old cars that his dad restored in his spare time. Mike's dad was an auto mechanic for a local GM dealership and while not a wealthy man, he made a better than average living with good benefits. The two enjoyed being together and Mike could tell his dad took special pride in teaching him some of the tricks of the trade. Mike took special pride in his dad when he learned that his dad was ranked in the top ten in a statewide auto mechanics test.

One afternoon when Mike was seventeen, he arrived home from school to find the phone ringing. On the other end of the line one of his father's friends told him in a gruff, gentle voice that his dad had been killed in an auto accident. Two years later, still not over the loss of his father, Mike learned that his mom had been diagnosed with breast cancer and would need surgery. He was devastated when the doctors came out of the operating room to inform him that his mom had died during the operation. For months afterward, when Mike saw or heard something that reminded him of one or both his parents, his eyes would fill with tears.

At nineteen, Mike was all-alone. His parents had been only children, like him, so he had no aunts or uncles or cousins. He had never known his grandparents, who had died when he was an infant. He supported himself with the money he had received from his father's life insurance policy, and the sixteen thousand dollars his father had left him—his dad's life savings, accumulated through years of frugal living.

After he graduated from high school Mike decided he didn't want to go to college. Studying had never come easy to him. He got a job at a Providence trucking company, and over the next year or so worked himself into an office position classifying freight. Like his dad, Mike was a simple man content with a satisfying job that paid a decent wage and had great benefits. Two years later, when a large national firm bought out the Providence company, Mike was given the opportunity to transfer to Dallas, where they needed good people. He had no ties or family in Providence and they offered him a nice raise in salary, so he jumped at it. Besides the long, cold winters were starting to get to him. In Dallas he bought season tickets to the Cowboys games and went hunting and fishing whenever he could. He lived alone, and that suited him just fine.

At the juncture of the interstate and the two-lane road that would take him to the lake, Mike pulled off the highway to stop at a convenience store he had visited several times on previous trips to the lake. He needed to pick up enough beer and food to get him through his three-day stay. It was about 10:30 in the morning Friday, November 22, 2003. As Mike pulled into the parking area, he noticed a couple of seedy-looking characters with long, disheveled hair standing off to the side of the store. He wondered what they were doing there, hanging out in a parking lot in the middle of the morning. Getting out of his car and walking toward the store, he sized them up and estimated they were perhaps in their late teens. They wore similar clothing, each in the same red and black and gray color. Were they members of some gang? Mike knew little or nothing about kids like these, or what drove them to join together in gangs.

When Mike was about fifteen feet from the entrance to the store, one of the young men walked up to him and pulled a gun from beneath his shirt. "Give me your money," the gunman demanded, his voice low but amazingly confident.

Mike's heart began to pound as he struggled to remain calm. "Now take it easy," Mike demanded in a tone that was meant to hide the fear he felt from head to toe but it was taken by the gunman as authoritative and threatening. Mike had just cashed his check the night before and had about four hundred dollars on him, money he was carrying in case he needed it during his fishing trip.

He could see how nervous the gunman was but he was just a kid, perhaps eighteen or nineteen, and though he seemed nervous, he didn't look like he actually wanted to hurt anyone. Mike decided to resist, and to try to reason with the youngster before handing over his hard-earned money.

"Now look, we can work this out," Mike said.

Without any hesitation the gunman now obviously annoyed and nervous to the point of shaking shot back, "Look man, there's nothing to work out. Just give me your money!" He pointed the gun at Mike's head. "Give me your money now or I'll shoot you man!" he warned, his voice ratcheting up in volume. Before Mike could even respond, the nervous young gunman shot him in the head at point-blank range. Mike's body went limp as he collapsed and fell to the ground.

"Why did you do that?" Mike muttered, in a barely recognizable tone, as he lay sprawled on the ground bleeding, in a semiconscious condition. In a blurry sense of reality he watched as the gunman ran off without a dime. Mortally wounded he sensed that he had lost control of his body, but he didn't feel much pain. As he lay there hoping someone would help him, his mind began to drift. He began to have flash backs of the memories he cherished, the fishing and hunting trips with his dad, and the memories of his mother who had tried so hard, though not successfully, to make his life complete after the divorce.

As he began to lose consciousness, Mike could faintly hear someone calling the police on a cell phone. He was still partly awake as he was loaded onto a stretcher, and was aware that he was being transported to the trauma hospital, Parkland Memorial. It was 11:15 AM when Mike's unconscious body arrived at the hospital and the doctors began working on him. By now he had lost an enormous amount of blood, and it didn't look like he was going to make it. The doctors did all they could for him, but Mike had suffered from a lack of oxygen to the brain, and there was no hope of recovery. The doctors were obligated to put him on a respirator until they could reach a relative, or a judge if no relatives could be found, to authorize removing him from it. They tried calling the only telephone number he had in his possession but got no answer so they wheeled Mike's lifeless body off to the side and waited for clearance to pronounce him dead, the truth be known they were hoping he would just stop breathing naturally.

In their relatively brief two-hundred-year history as a nation, Americans have seen several presidents assassinated. From the beginning of time, those with wealth and power, regardless of their popularity as leaders, have had to live with one eye focused on those who would take that wealth and power from them. Sons have killed fathers and uncles; wives have poisoned their husbands and used their feminine wiles to seduce men with wealth or power. The annals of history are riddled with stories of generals and politicians who would risk everything to overthrow their king or ruler. It has long been said that power corrupts, and absolute power corrupts absolutely. How could anyone have known that Mike Reardon was about to play a major role in the history of the United States? How could anyone have known that at 12:31 PM, events that would have a profound affect on the entire nation would begin to unfold?

CHAPTER 2

▼

THE BEGINNING OF THE END

Facing the prospect of a close election contest in less than a year, John Francis Kelley, the President of the United States, had been persuaded by Vice President Lincoln B. Jones to make a trip to the vice president's home state of Texas. The purpose of the visit was to mend fences in the South, a key part of Kelley's election strategy. In the first several years of his presidency, John Kelley had made several controversial decisions that didn't play well in the Bible-Belt South. He tried to have it both ways by publicly opposing legislation in several state legislatures but then he sent in legislative aids to work out compromises that allowed the legislation to become laws in those states. In several states he opposed legislation that would have given gay partners new legal rights they heretofore did not enjoy, but he did so in such a non-committed approach that the legislation passed.

For one piece of state legislation allowing gay marriage, he did little more than provide moral support. He was seen in the South as not standing up more forcefully for the religious principals the South dearly cherished. Given the fact that he was a moderate Republican from the heavily Democratic liberal state of Massachusetts, his political strategists thought visiting the hostile Texas environment might play well in the national press. Besides, his VP was pushing hard for this visit to Dallas. During his trip, the president would give a major speech to Dallas businessmen and politicians about the sharp and growing divisions among the American people. He was genuinely concerned that these deep divisions were tearing the country apart. In the last national election, the popular vote had been amazingly close, coming down to just a few hundred votes out of about fifty million.

On November 22, 2003, at 12:31 PM, shots were fired at the president of the United States as he toured downtown Dallas in an open limousine. The president and his wife, Jackie, were sitting in the back of the car, the governor and his wife in the front.

The president's motorcade sped toward Parkland Hospital with the badly wounded president. Several members of the president's staff arrived at the hospital moments before the limo. Special Presidential Assistants Kenny O'Donnell and Larry O'Brien had been with the president since the early days, when John F. Kelley was first elected to Congress. Along with Bobby, the president's brother, and Dave Powell, they were part of the inner circle of the president's closest friends, a group affectionately, and sometimes not so affectionately, called the Irish mafia.

Expecting the president's limo to arrive at the hospital at any moment, O'Donnell took charge; he instructed police and emergency room personnel to clear the halls and keep everyone away from the room they would bring the president into. Anxious to make contact with the president's brother, O'Donnell placed a call to Bobby Kelley at his Virginia farm. Bobby had been getting ready to leave town on official Justice Department business, but had heard the news flashes and was beside himself not knowing what was going on. All he knew from the news reports was that shots had been fired at the president and that he had been hit at least once.

"Hi Bobby, I'm at the hospital. Have you been listening to the news?" O'Donnell asked.

"Of course I have, Kenny. What in the world is going on? What can you tell me about my brother's condition? Is he alive? How badly was he wounded?"

"I'm still waiting for Jack's limo to get here. It should only be another minute or two," O'Donnell reported. Bobby instructed him to keep the phone line open, so he could be kept abreast of his brother's condition once the limo arrived at the hospital.

Just a few moments before O'Donnell's call, FBI Director Jay E. Howard had called Bobby. Without offering any condolence, Howard tersely stated that "the president has been shot, and I've just learned that he has died." Bobby thought it strange that Howard had such information, when he knew now that he had an open line to Kenny O'Donnell, that the president had not yet arrived at the hospital. Howard's cold demeanor was startling given the highly emotional state Bobby was in.

"Are you sure?" Bobby blurted out to Howard. "The reports are that Jack is still in transit to the hospital."

Howard, now anxious to end the conversation, told Bobby, "I've got to go Mr. Kelley, my phones are ringing off the hook." He then abruptly hung up. Over the next few weeks, despite the fact that Bobby in his position as Attorney General was Howard's boss, with their offices on the same floor at the Justice Department just a few dozen feet apart, Howard never offered any sign of condolence over the next several weeks. Later, reflecting on the events of that day, Bobby recognized that Howard didn't realize when he placed his call to Bobby that he was ahead of the curve.

With his secret files on just about everyone who was anyone in Washington politics, Howard had enjoyed decades of unopposed challenge to his authority at the FBI, the world's premier law enforcement agency. That all ended when Jack took the Presidential Oath of Office and Bobby became attorney general. Howard was accustomed to the prestige of nearly unlimited access to the president and to the highest levels of government, but Bobby had restricted Howard in that access. That was only one of the reasons Howard had grown to hate the president and his brother over the past several years.

"Could his hatred of the president have led him to gloat and call prematurely? Could he have had a hand in the shooting?" Bobby thought. "How could anyone have known the president was dead before he even arrived at the hospital? Was it just wishful thinking, or did he know something?"

For what seemed like an eternity, Bobby was anxiously beside himself, pacing back and forth, as he waited for O'Donnell to come back on the open line to tell him his brother's limousine had arrived at the hospital. Bobby's mind began to wander, as he reminisced about their youth. Jack was 9 years older than him, so they were not very close in their early childhood years, but they had made up for that as adults. They were now totally loyal to each other and inseparable. Their flamboyant father, Joe, had graduated from Harvard Business School years before, and with his substantial donations to Harvard, each of the brothers followed in his footsteps. They were each admitted to Harvard and then went on to graduate from Harvard Law School.

As his brother's campaign manager in both his Senate races and his presidential race, Robert F. Kelley was politically astute. He earned a reputation for being absolutely ruthless, and was certainly his father's son when it came to dealing with the competition. Joe Kelley, who in his early twenties was a self-made multi-millionaire, had deservedly earned the reputation for being reckless and ruthless. Bobby never took on a fight to lose, winning was not everything it was the only thing. He had learned well from his father and had no qualms about being single-mindedly ruthless when dealing with those he considered his enemy. Jack knew that with his brother in charge of his election efforts, he could stand above the fray and stay on message, while behind the scenes Bobby did whatever it took to destroy his opponent.

In 2000, when he decided to run for the presidency, John Francis Kelley had a difficult opponent. His Democratic challenger, Richard Dixon was a sitting vice president with the blessing of a popular president under whom he had served for the previous eight years. JFK was an unusual Republican, a fiscal conservative in a state that was openly very liberal and that had a long history of voting for liberal Democrats. With his strange mix of liberal socialism and fiscal conservatism, Kelley had been elected to congress in two congressional elections and two senatorial elections.

Massachusetts had a national reputation for electing the most liberal of politicians. For many years the Democratic Party at all levels of state and local government had been left leaning, supporting liberal special interest groups. Kelley was an anomaly in Massachusetts, and he would have to prove himself on a national level. He was a Republican when a national majority of registered voters were Democrats. He was Roman Catholic, and only one other Catholic had ever run for the presidency. That candidate, Al Smith, had lost. As if those odds against Kelley winning national office were not enough, the economy had been going gangbusters for eight years under the existing administration, and Vice President Dixon could, although undeservedly, take credit for it. With the House and Senate being Republican, neither he nor the president had much to do with the policies that made the economy strong.

When the presidential limo arrived at Parkland Hospital, several hospital attendants lifted the president's limp, unconscious body onto a stretcher. They also attended to the governor lifting him onto another stretcher. The Governor's wounds to the shoulder, arm, and leg, while serious were not life threatening. The vice president's limo arrived seconds later. Vice President Jones was visibly shaken as he watched the doctors and nurses rush the president's lifeless body inside the emergency room doors, blood everywhere.

"OK Bobby, he's here," O'Donnell hollered into the phone. "Just hang on, all hell is breaking loose here. I'll come back to you as soon as I know something concrete." In the few minutes since the shots had rung out, a large crowd had gathered outside the emergency room entrance. It was immediately apparent to everyone watching that the president's wounds were very serious. The president was bleeding profusely from a neck wound, and one side of his head was covered in blood and appeared devoid of hair. His white dress shirt was bright red and soaked in blood, and his normally well-groomed chestnut-colored hair was crimson.

O'Donnell followed as the president was wheeled the down a hall and into the nearest room, where a team of eight doctors and three nurses immediately surrounded him. Listening to the doctors bark out their orders—"Prepare to intubate! Start an IV of morphine and saline!"—O'Donnell learned that the first bullet had hit the president in the head, immediately knocking him unconscious. But the bullet had not hit him square in the head, it grazed his head. Just a quarter inch closer and it would have completely shattered his skull. Yet the bullet cut a swath of scalp and bone, from its' point of impact the length of the president's head and opened up the skin as if it were being filleted, bursting blood vessels and scraping a deep groove in his skull. Whether he would live or die would be in the hands of these talented physicians.

"Bobby, it doesn't look good. There's blood everywhere. Jack is unconscious and not responding."

"Is he alive?" Bobby shouted, trying to speak over the background noise he heard coming over the line.

"I don't know, Bobby. They're working on him, and I just don't know. "It doesn't look good."

The president's neck wound was also very serious. The first shot to the head had caused him to jerk to the right. The next bullet hit him in the neck, entering at an angle from the president's left. It tore thru the muscle and exited beneath his Adam's apple, nicking his windpipe and tearing a two-and-a-half inch hole in the lower part of his neck As O'Donnell listened to the doctors call out medical orders, giving orders for this procedure or that procedure, he relayed what he was hearing to the president's brother. It would be twenty minutes before Bobby knew his brother was still alive and had a chance, however slim, to live. As the tears welled up in his eyes all Bobby could think was, "Who could have done this? Was there another shoe to drop? Was he himself a target?" The United States was under attack, and no one knew from where it was coming or what the assassins had in mind for the next stage of their bloody coup.

"Kenny, can you hear me? Kenny, are you there?"

"Yes, Bobby. I'm here."

"Kenny, I want you to secure the entire area. Everyone, but I mean everyone, including and perhaps especially the vice president and his entire Secret Service detail, must be cleared away from the area. No exceptions other than the doctors and two or three of the president's most trusted bodyguards." O'Donnell added, "And Kenny, make sure they are armed to the teeth. Kenny listen to me once the area is cleared; no one is to have any communication with the outside unless it is cleared through you. Robert Kelley was nervous but clearheaded as he continued to rattle off his thoughts to his friend Kenny O'Donnell.

"If my brother does have a chance to live through this, I didn't want some assassin team walking into the emergency room to finish their botched murder of the president. Imagine the balls of these guys, Kenny, trying to kill my brother and take over the United States."

Bobby was known for his ability to think clearly in crisis situations. As he continued to instruct O'Donnell, he tried to focus on the possible mindset of those responsible for the assassination attempt. "Kenny, whoever did this must be led to believe that their mission was successful," Bobby explained. "Whether Jack lives or not, I want to know who did this and how deep the conspiracy goes. If the conspirators believe the president is in fact dead, they might become more emboldened and might tip their hand. These were not some run-of-the-mill criminals." Even at this early stage of events, Bobby sensed his brother's shooting had the scent of something coming from the highest levels of government.

"Kenny this may sound cold," Bobby continued, "but do you agree that for now we must assume the worst and pretend that Jack is not only not going to make it, but in fact that he is already clinically dead?"

"I agree, Bobby," O'Donnell said. "Whoever did this must be led to believe they were successful. Who knows what they are capable of, or for that matter what they'd do if they thought they would be exposed."

"Kenny, you're the man at the point on this, and I have every confidence in you to pull this off," Bobby said.

Kenny O'Donnell was the president's special assistant for political matters, and was in the loop on almost everything that went on with the president. In fact, O'Donnell was the president's "gatekeeper." Few people got to see the president without clearing it with O'Donnell first. He knew well that the president had, for the past year, been involved in some very controversial political decisions. These decisions involved major military cutbacks that would change the way the country fought wars. In fact, the president was convinced that by redirecting the enormous Defense Department budget to newer, more technically advanced military weapons; he could develop a technologically superior military that no other nation on earth could match. That would mean that some of the "sacred cows" of the military would be phased out and cut from the budget, and there were a lot of powerful people who wouldn't like that.

The president was about to redirect hundreds of billions of dollars per year to military technology that had only been embraced at the Pentagon by a small group of younger generals and admirals. This wouldn't sit well with the hundreds of retired high-ranking officers now employed by huge multibillion-dollar defense contractors, or with current military officers, who owed their status to their retired predecessors, who offered these contractors privileged treatment. It would disrupt their arrangement, the continuous cycle of favored treatment that resulted in big defense contracts and added billions of dollars to each defense contractors' bottom line.

Of course whenever one of these Pentagon officials retired and left the employ of government, they were welcomed with open arms with very generous "consulting contracts" by the CEO's of these billion dollar defense contractor corporations. President Dwight D. Eisenhower in his farewell address at the end of his second term as President first coined the phrase and described these corporations as the "Military Industrial Complex" and warned of their growing power and influence over the defense of our country. He went on to say *"the total influence-economic, political, even spiritual—is felt in every city, every Statehouse, every office of the Federal government. The potential for the disastrous rise of misplaced power exists. We must never let the weight of this combination…of power, endanger our liberties or democratic processes. Only an alert and knowledgeable citizenry can compel the proper meshing of the huge industrial and military machinery of defense with our peaceful methods and goals, so that security and liberty may prosper together."*

At several meetings the president had called to plan these far-reaching changes, a number of high-ranking generals and Defense Department officials had voiced veiled threats against the president. O'Donnell and Bobby wanted the president to pass these threats on to the Secret Service, but the president shrugged the threats off, likening them to "a bunch of kids who had their ball taken away during a ball game by a bigger kid."

These very same generals had had an open and public split with administration officials during preparations to invade Afghanistan a year and a half before the assassination attempt. The president believed he could resolve the problem with the ruling Afghan Taliban party politically, and he had begun a dialogue with them through the UN and Pakistan. The military saw this as open defiance—the Taliban had given sanctuary to the Islamic terrorists who had attacked the United States in its own backyard. On September 11, 2001, just eight months after the president took office; the United States had been attacked by a group of Islamic terrorists operating out of Afghanistan. These terrorists hijacked commercial airplanes and flew them into the World Trade Center and the Pentagon, killing thousands of U.S. citizens. These terrorists seemed to have the open support of the Afghan government, which was run by an Islamic fundamentalist group called the Taliban.

A number of U.S. military leaders simply wanted to destroy the Taliban through military force, but the president, knowing full well that the military would have little trouble accomplishing this goal, wanted to keep the military option open but first attempt to get the Taliban to release those responsible for the terrorist attacks. Most of the military leaders who opposed the president's military modernization efforts believed the U.S. needed to have, at its core, divisions of heavy armor, tank divisions at maximum strength, and large infantry divisions to mobilize and take the fight to the Taliban.

The president, along with a number of very forward-thinking one-and two-star generals and several lower-ranking admirals, believed the armed forces of the future needed to be highly technical, with special forces that had quick strike capabilities using overwhelming lethal force. The president wanted a military that could subdue its opponents with the use of overwhelming force through air strikes with laser-guided precision bombs. Moving large tank divisions could take months, so the president wanted a substantially more mobile tank force that could be moved by transport planes. This tank force would be so technically superior that two or three dozen of the military's latest tanks, bolstered by ground and air support, would be nearly invincible. Fast-moving, highly mobile special force troops on the ground, connected by satellite to air and sea power, would be at the core of this new military power.

The senior-ranking generals who were still thinking in terms of Second World War military strategy believed the United States should have answered the terrorist attacks with a massive military buildup and invasion. The president overruled them, and they didn't like it. He not only overruled them, he appointed some of his loyal officers to head up projects designed to redirect money and energy needed to accomplish his goal of modernizing the military.

Under the president's new military command structure, the officers the president would now rely upon were for the most part in their thirties and forties, were trained in computer sciences and were spearheading the technological changes in the military. To assure their independence in these matters from some of their senior officers they were to report directly to the Assistant Secretary of

Defense. Through Kenny O'Donnell, these officers would have access to the president. They were not to follow their normal chain of command. These senior-ranking officers felt the president would unnecessarily expose the United States to a failed military engagement and produce worldwide embarrassment. The generals and the CIA were still smarting from the humiliating defeat they had suffered a decade before, when liberal politicians gutted the defense and intelligence budgets and then made them the scapegoat for all that went wrong in the world. They longed for the year when they could have a Commander in Chief that they could trust, and they despised this rich kid, who they believed stole the presidency from Richard Dixon.

After several minutes O'Donnell picked up the phone again. "Bobby, it's really crazy here. I need to get going on some of the things we've talked about. I can tell you that Jack is still alive! The doctors are still working feverishly on him. If he were dead, they'd have given up by now."

"OK, Kenny I'll let you go," Bobby said, his voice shaking, "but call me the minute anything changes for better or worse, and let me know what I can do from this side."

After O'Donnell hung up the phone, the wounded president just a dozen or so feet away, O'Donnell called over several Secret Service agents he knew he could trust. He quietly told two of the agents the president was still alive and asked for their cooperation in keeping it a secret. "I don't know exactly where we are going with this yet but we suspect that if the assassins knew the president was alive they would make another attempt on his life", O'Donnell explained. "Until we know who is behind this I would ask that you not share this information with anyone else and that includes the other members of your Secret Service detail" O'Donnell added. He instructed one of them to go to the emergency room lobby, where the vice president was still waiting, and tell him the president had been pronounced dead.

While the vice president readied himself to go back to the airport and the capitol, O'Donnell simultaneously called an impromptu news conference in front of the entrance to the hospital. The vice president's limo was just driving off when he ordered the car to stop so he could hear what O'Donnell was saying. In a short statement, speaking somberly, O'Donnell announced, "I have just been informed by the lead emergency room doctor that President John Kelley has died from his wounds. I am told the president did not suffer very long and probably never knew what hit him." He said to the reporters, "Please bear with me during this trying time. I will shortly arrange to have one or more of the doctors who treated the president speak with you to be sure you all get the details as they became available."

O'Donnell then went back inside and pulled the lead doctor aside. "Doc, you know who I am, don't you? I need you to level with me, tell me like it is. Is the president going to make it?"

Dr. Clark, a man in his mid-thirties, said, "Yes, I know who you are Mr. O'Donnell I know that you were one of the president's best friends, and I'm truly sorry this happened. I can tell you the wounds are very serious and life threatening. It will be hours before I can say for certain, but I'm optimistic at this point. I can assure you that the entire team will work tirelessly and use all our skill to save the president."

"Thank you Doc," O'Donnell said, "we all appreciate what you and your team are doing."

As O'Donnell started to walk away, the doctor said, "I voted for President Kelley last time, and I'm going to do everything in my power to see that I'll be able to vote for him again. Have they caught the people who shot the president?"

"Not yet doc," O'Donnell replied, "but I'm sure the FBI is already working on it."

O'Donnell, taking several steps back toward the doctor, leaned closer so only he could hear what he was about to say. "You must know that whoever attempted this assassination are powerful people who were attempting to take over the government of the United States. Doc, it is extremely important that you and your medical colleagues allow the rest of the world to believe that those responsible for this assassination were successful and that the president died".

O'Donnell continued, "If the assassins know the president is still alive, they will almost certainly make another attempt to get the job done, and who knows how many people would die in a second attempt to kill the president. Such an attempt would no doubt be one that ensured that everyone in the general area would not live through it."

O'Donnell asked, "Doctor, have you ever served in the armed forces?"

"I served an eight-year tour of duty in the Marines and left as a major," the doctor said. "Five of the attending physicians now working on the president have also served in the military. In fact, two of the three nurses served in the Navy."

"These doctors and nurses most probably didn't know who I am, but they know you well and respect you Dr. Clark. Would you explain the urgency of having their cooperation in keeping the failed assassination of the president totally secret until friends of the president notified them otherwise?

"After you have this confidential conversation with each of your medical team, I'm going to ask that you step outside and address the waiting news media regarding the medical reasons for the president's death. And, Doc, please make it convincing. I have already told them that the president had been pronounced dead, and I need you to back that up with a medical briefing."

Smiling, Dr. Clark replied, "Do you mind if I call you Kenny?" "Please do. That's what my friends call me."

As Dr. Clark walked away he turned and said, "You're a good man, Kenny. Thank you for asking me to help you with this. Trust me, I'll make it convincing."

O'Donnell asked one of the Secret Service agents to order a casket and have it delivered to the ER. Then he went back inside to find the first lady. Jackie had never uttered a word and never left the president's side. O'Donnell had become good friends with the first lady over the years and considered her a totally loyal and immensely strong person. She was certainly holding up well under the incredible pressure of this unbelievable day.

O'Donnell spoke softly to her, consoling her, and assured her, "Jackie, I've just had a conversation with Dr. Clark. He said he thinks Jack has an excellent chance to pull through this. I've been in touch with Bobby, and we both agree that until we learn more about who might have been behind this, we want everyone to think that Jack didn't make it. We're afraid that if they thought they missed killing Jack, they might make another attempt, and Jack is in no shape to be moved. Besides, we aren't sure who we could trust or where we could safely move him to.

"Bobby and I are sure that this is a conspiracy, more than likely one at the highest levels of government. Jack would be in constant danger until he recovered sufficiently."

Jackie agreed. "Kenny, I trust you and Bobby completely. I'll do whatever you want of me, anything so Jack will recover from this."

Outside the emergency room entrance, Dr. Clark stood at a hastily set up portable microphone and announced, "I have been asked to make a statement regarding the president's cause of death, after which I will take some of your questions."

"Several resuscitative measures were attempted," Clark continued, "including the use of oxygen, anesthesia, an endiotracheal tube, a tracheotomy, and blood and fluids were administered. By the time the president arrived at the hospital he was already critically ill. It was apparent the president had sustained two very serious wounds. A missile had gone in and out of the back of his head causing external lacerations and a loss of brain tissue." He continued, "The president lost his heart action by electrocardiogram. A closed-chest cardiograph massage was administered, as were other emergency resuscitation measures. The president was pronounced dead at 1 PM Central Time," Dr. Clark concluded.

The questions from the reporters were relentless. They wanted every detail about the wounds. "How many shots hit the president?" "Where did they hit him?" "What kind of gun was used?" "Did the president suffer before he died?" "Was Jackie OK?" "Where was she?" "Would the president's body be taken back to Washington?" "Had anyone been in touch with the president's brother?" "How was the Governor?" "Would he survive?" "Had the assassins been caught?" "Who did he think was behind this?" "Was there only one assassin?" "Where was the vice president? Was he OK?"

Watching the press conference on television, Bobby wasn't completely sure that this announcement wasn't the real thing. He kept telling himself Kenny would have called him if it were. Dr. Clark had done an absolutely convincing job.

CHAPTER 3

▼

DECEIVING THE DECEIVERS

As Dr. Clark came back inside the hospital after the news conference, he called O'Donnell over and confidentially whispered, "Kenny, I don't know if this makes any sense, but we have another trauma patient who was brought in just a few hours earlier with a gunshot wound to the head. That patient had been removed from life support and died just ten minutes prior to the president's arrival. If the president does live, perhaps the other patient's body might be of use in keeping secret that the president was alive, at least until the president is out of danger."

"What's this guy's name?" O'Donnell asked. "Was he married, did he have known relatives to claim the body? What blood type is he? Can I see him?"

Dr. Clark brought O'Donnell into a holding area for deceased patients, and O'Donnell viewed the lifeless body of Mike Reardon. Astonished, O'Donnell noted that he was the same height and roughly the same weight and build as the president. Even his hair was a chestnut color like the president's. Mike Reardon had been shot point blank with a large-caliber weapon, so there was tremendous damage to his head. Because he had lived for several hours after his attack, his heart still pumping blood, his face had swollen to the point that his facial features were extremely distorted. Even close friends would not have recognized him.

"Do their blood types match, doc?" "Yes, Kenny. Even their blood types match."

O'Donnell wondered, "Can I pull this off? Would someone come looking for Reardon and blow this whole thing wide open?" O'Donnell asked the doctor for all the personal effects in Reardon's possession when they brought him in.

"How in the world can we fool the government doctors who might want to perform an autopsy?" O'Donnell said.

"Kenny, they're not going to be looking at the possibility that this guy isn't the president," the doctor said. "They won't do DNA tests, and even if they do it will be weeks before they get the test results back. I think you can pull this off. The autopsy will likely be a sham, especially if this whole thing is a conspiracy as we both think."

O'Donnell made a mental note to be sure to tell Bobby that he had to use every political favor available to dissuade whoever might wish to from doing an autopsy. In fact, he had to somehow get word to Bobby that he was going to substitute Reardon's body for Jack's. That would be no easy task. He was sure that those responsible for this act of treason would be monitoring everything coming out of Dallas for days, or at least until they felt secure that their mission was accomplished.

Vice President Jones left the hospital with the Dallas Chief of Police, Joe Sewell; a congressman named Michael Smith; and his Secret Service detail as soon as it was announced that the president was dead, and headed immediately for Air Force One. On the way to the airport, he called for a federal judge to administer the presidential oath of office, not just any federal judge but one he had been instrumental in having appointed to the bench. He also made a call for photographers to come to Air Force One, and then instructed Secret Service agents to go to Air Force Two and remove his and the second lady's clothing and personal effects and bring them over to Air Force One. He then called Bobby, his Attorney General. Bobby never did get along with the Vice President. Jones knew that Bobby had done everything in his power to dissuade Jack from selecting him to be his running mate. The last few years Bobby had made sure the vice president's access to the president was substantially limited. There was no love lost between these two men.

"Bobby, it's Lincoln. I'm at a loss for words to tell you how sorry I am. I want you to know that I am going to do everything within my power to bring whoever did this to justice. Tell me, is there anything I can do for you?"

Bobby sensed almost immediately an attitude of smugness and superiority in Jones' voice. He was sure the bastard had something to do with Jack's assassination attempt, but he didn't know exactly what form his involvement took. Bobby vowed that if the vice president was involved, he would get even with him. He swore he would do whatever it took to find those responsible, even if he had to spend millions of dollars of his father's fortune.

"Thank you, Lincoln," Bobby responded, "we are all still in shock."

Bobby was concerned about his sister-in-law. "How is Jackie holding up?" he asked.

"We're waiting for her to arrive with the casket. She insisted that she would not leave here without Jack" the VP volunteered. "Bobby, I want you to know that I have sent for a federal judge and that I will be sworn in as president in the next few minutes. Is there any constitutional reason this would be inappropriate?"

Bobby hesitated for a moment. Collecting his thoughts, he realized that Lincoln B. Jones, a man he'd never trusted or liked, was about to become the president of the United States.

"No, Mr. President," he said, nearly choking on the word, "I don't believe there is any language regarding the appropriate timing for a new president to be sworn in after a president dies while in office."

As he hung up the phone he began to realize that the kind of proof he would have to present to a court of law about these assassins would probably never materialize. These guys dared attempting to pull off a coup d'e.tat on the president of the United States; they would never leave the kind of evidence that could be tied to them directly. In fact, he reasoned, the guys who were the actual triggermen had probably already been killed.

So what would he do with these assassins, and how could he be sure of who they were and how far the conspiracy went? His mind quickly drifted from one thought to another, but one thing he was sure of, this assassination attempt could not have happened without the knowledge of CIA and FBI and perhaps high-ranking military officers from the DIA, or Defense Intelligence Agency. O'Donnell later discovered that the president's route had been altered at the last minute. Who could have done this? The new route brought the presidential limousine closer to the shooters and made a sharp left-hand turn that ensured the car was traveling at a slower speed as it passed the shooters.

Bobby knew from planning previous trips that only the Secret Service could change the president's route. Whoever had changed Jack's route was definitely involved somehow. Bobby would later learn that nearly every rule of presidential travel had been broken. Windows along the route were allowed to be opened, and the limo was an open-top convertible, which was unheard of. How could they have allowed such a car? The escort police were well behind the president's limo rather than beside it, and the VP was in a car just two vehicles behind the president. It was a security nightmare. Anyone, who remotely covered up the obvious truth, would have to be involved somehow in this conspiracy.

Shortly after Dr. Clark's news conference announcing the president's death Bobby received a call from O'Donnell and Larry O'Brien on a secure line.

Ken and Larry had agreed before they called that they could not chance telling Bobby about Reardon, even on a secure line.

"I wanted to bring you up to speed on what's going on here," O'Donnell said. "We have arranged to have the president's body brought back in the casket." Bobby wasn't sure what to think. Jack wasn't dead, what were they talking about?

"Also Bobby, we had a little ruckus with the local authorities. They wanted to keep the body and perform an autopsy, but we insisted that we were taking the body back to Washington with us. I'll fill you in when I see you in a few hours."

Alone again with his thoughts Bobby completely trusted his two friends. Whatever they were doing would be just fine. But his dark side, that side of him that sought revenge, continued to crowd his thoughts, and he could only focus on getting even with whoever was responsible for trying to kill his brother.

Several years before Jack became president, Bobby had been appointed chief counsel to the Senate Labor Rackets Committee. The main thrust of the investigation was to determine the extent to which the Mob had control of the nation's unions. Most of these behind–the-scenes people were members of the Italian Mob. Bobby recalled with amazement how he would subpoena people to testify against some high-ranking union official, only to learn that they had succumbed to fatal heart attacks, or were in serious auto crashes, or had simply disappeared. Later, as Attorney General, he had indicted over three hundred and fifty known Mafia leaders, even though he knew that prior to Jack's presidential primaries, his father had made a deal with Mob leaders that involved major union support for Jack. In return their father promised his sons would turn their heads on Mob-related activity after Jack was elected. Somehow Jack and Bobby never felt bound by their father's promise, even though they knew full well that they won the election because of their father's deal with the Mob. The Mob was furious at their betrayal.

As Bobby thought about how these street people dealt with their enemies, he began to formulate a plan for dealing with those individuals behind the conspiracy. He couldn't help but wonder if some of these Mafia people could have been angry enough to involve themselves in Jack's assassination attempt. If that were the case, it meant that these people were part of the conspiracy. Bobby realized that if in fact the Italian Mob had something to do with his brother's attack, he was up against a very formidable group of men who had the power of government and the ruthlessness of street killers. Nonetheless, he could think of nothing else but teaching all of them a lesson. No one was going to get away with doing something like this to his family without paying a severe price.

Even before the casket arrived aboard Air Force One with Jackie and the others, Bobby had hours to think about the whole matter. He was almost certain that those involved would turn out to be political enemies. But then again he was certain that somehow they were also connected to the military, After all, he reasoned, Jack had been shaking up the military establishment from the time he took office. "Could all these various enemy factions have somehow come together to join forces to do away with their common enemy?" Bobby wondered. Thinking rationally he tried to dismiss the idea—it was a little farfetched—but it kept creeping back into his thoughts, and it haunted him to think he was up against such powerful enemies.

On October 11, just six weeks before his attempted assassination, the president had signed a top-secret memo to the Secretary of State, the Secretary of Defense, and the Joint Chiefs of Staff, with copies to the CIA director and the Administrator Agency for International Development. The memo was quite detailed. The president directed that *no formal announcement be made of the implementation of plans to reduce the size of military personnel throughout the world.* The implementation was to begin before the end of that year.

On October 29th less than a month before the assassination, the president signed another memo and sent it to the same recipients, directing them that *this memo should not be discussed publicly, nor with our allies.* The president's memo went on to outline the following military initiatives:

1. The three C-130 squadrons permanently stationed in France will be returned to the United States within eight months, as scheduled.

2. U.S. Army lines of communication forces in France will be reduced by 5,400.

3. Inactivation of the Lacrosse and 280mm gun battalions will proceed as scheduled.

4. A plan for further reorganization of the Army's European logistics forces, entailing an additional reduction of about 30,000 personnel over the next two calendar years.

5. The specific 10 percent reduction in headquarters staff of the 7th Army and USAREUR and the overall 15 percent reduction worldwide in headquarters staffs…will go forward as scheduled.

6. The president approved the return to the United States, commencing early next year, and to be completed by late that year, with minimum explanation as practicable, the six Berlin Roundout units consisting of three artillery battalions, two armored battalions, and one cavalry regiment with all its support units.

7. The redeployment of the second Long Thrust battle group will not be discussed until January, although planning should go forward for its probable return to the United States by early next spring.

8. B-47 units will be withdrawn from Spain and the United Kingdom…by spring one year hence. The president reaffirmed this decision after being informed that the Joint Chiefs of Staff were against this action.

9. The president approved in principle the proposal to withdraw three fighter squadrons from France and seven fighter squadrons from the United Kingdom no later than December two years hence.

It had been at least seven or eight months since the recipients of this memo had met with the president and learned of his intention to start reducing the U.S. military, so they would have had plenty of time to plan his murder and the ensuing cover-up.

It was difficult to minimize the animosity that developed between the Joint Chiefs and President Kelley, Robert Kelley and members of the Kelley staff. There were several meetings where the generals' tone of voice was so hostile; the president's aids considered asking some of the Secret Service men to step into the room. Given the enormity of these presidential directives for military cutbacks, it was not difficult to conceive of their complicity in the assassination and its cover-up.

"But how could any of this happen without the CIA or FBI getting some wind of it?" Bobby reasoned that the CIA, and FBI, and DIA either knew about the assassination and participated in it or did nothing to stop it, either of which was unthinkable.

"Either way" Bobby thought, "this bastard Jay E. Howard had Jack's blood on his hands. He had to be involved." Yet he couldn't dismiss the nagging thought that the Mob was involved somehow. He had investigated many Mob-related killings and instinctively knew that this assassination had all the earmarks of a Mob hit. For the first time he began to fear the enormity of what he might be up against. "As smart as we all have been, could we have totally missed this alliance of evil as it was formed against us?" Bobby asked himself.

Howard could be incredibly ruthless. He had been appointed FBI Director some twenty-eight years before, and it was well-known that he collected information on just about every member of Congress and anyone who was anyone. He used that information to its maximum potential when he threatened numerous politicians with a leak of certain information when he wanted political favors. The Kelleys and Howard had never gotten along. They hadn't liked each other from the very beginning. But Howard simply didn't have the balls to be directly involved, Bobby thought. He was ruthlessly corrupt, but he was not stupid. What few people knew was that for nineteen years Howard had lived immediately across the street from Vice President Jones. They frequently socialized together over dinner and cocktails, and over the years had become good friends. As Senate majority leader, Jones knew negative things about his political enemies that could only have come from Howard's FBI investigations.

Bobby didn't doubt for a moment that Howard probably would have sat on the fence collecting incriminating evidence on the assassination "players" for his files, all the while passively hoping for the demise of both Jack and Bobby Kelley. Years before, through their father's own dealings with the Italian Mob, the Kelleys had learned what most intelligence officials suspected but could not prove, that the Mob had absolute proof that Howard and his next in command at the FBI were homosexual lovers. Through the years whenever it suited their needs, the Mob would discreetly remind Howard of his own vulnerability. So if in fact Howard had stumbled upon certain suspicious activities related to Mob involvement in the assassination, he would never expose the people who with a few incriminating photos could ruin his career.

Knowing that he and his family and friends needed to be protected by someone he could absolutely trust, Bobby decided to place a call to a dear friend he had grown up with and attended Harvard with. Sean McDonald had graduated from Harvard in the top ten in his class. Upon graduation he enlisted in the Marines as a commissioned officer. He went through boot camp and was the kind of guy who excelled in everything he did. He was chosen to train at the Navy Seal school, finished in the top five of his group and then went on to train in the special forces and was part of the initial units sent into Afghanistan to guide the fall of the ruling Taliban.

Sean was surprised to hear from Bobby, especially after the announcement of the president's assassination.

"Sean, its Bobby Kelley." "Gee Bobby I'm so sorry to hear about Jack," he said. "I can't imagine what you are going through. I know how close you two were."

Sean had known the president for years before his election, but he was actually Bobby's friend, and with the nine-year age difference between Bobby and Jack, he hadn't socialized all that much with Jack.

"Sean thank you how's your wife and family"? Still with a deep tone of loss in his voice Sean responded "Just fine Bobby, can I be of any help, can I do anything for you?" Sean asked.

"There is something I would like to ask of you, Sean. I would like to meet with you as soon as possible."

Sean agreed to meet Jack the following Thursday, at 10 PM at the pancake house on K Street.

"Oh, and Sean, don't say a word of this to anyone. I not only want to ask you for help in several matters as a personal friend, I want you to know that this also involves national security of a very sensitive nature." Anyone who knew the Kelleys also knew of their friendship with McDonald; they would be highly suspicious of such an urgent meeting between Bobby and Sean. Bobby was reasonably sure that any surveillance that might have been placed on him before the assassination would now be relaxed, as those responsible had to be much more comfortable knowing the president was dead. Thinking it wise to be cautious, however, Bobby told Sean to make sure he took every precaution not to be followed.

It was nearly 7 PM by the time Air Force One arrived in Washington. Every major newspaper and TV station had assembled to record the return of the president's body. After the huge plane came to a stop, the large cargo bay doors were lowered and a ramp was rolled up to the plane. Bobby made his way up the ramp to join his sister-in-law, Jackie, and his friends at the side of the casket. Still in a daze and not completely sure what was happening, Jackie and several of the president's closest friends had sat beside the casket during the entire three-hour flight to Washington. Bobby embraced Jackie and kissed her on the cheek. She was still clothed in the bloodstained suit she had worn earlier that day. Bobby assured her that all would be well. His arms around her, he whispered in her ear, "I've just spoken to Dr. Clark at the hospital. He tells me that while there's no change in Jack's condition, that's a good sign. Jack is a fighter. If anyone can pull through this, he can. It's out of our hands now Jackie, these doctors are really talented, don't worry, Jack has many friends who are ready to step in and help, this is going to turn out just fine. I'm going to be there every step of the way."

Jackie's voice was fragile; as they hugged he could still feel Jackie's body shaking hours after the ordeal she had gone through. Her voice was weak as she said, "Bobby, Jones said he spoke with you and that you suggested he take the presidential oath of office before he left Dallas. He was in such a hurry. He had all his clothes and belongings carried onto our plane."

In less than an hour after he left Parkland hospital Jones had arranged to have all his personal effects moved from Air Force Two and brought to Air Force One. He had a Federal Judge, whom he nominated to the bench on board to administer the oath and had photographers there to record it. Bobby couldn't believe the story Jackie was telling him.

"I didn't suggest he take the oath in Dallas. He is a damn liar. Jackie, we are just going to have to go with the flow until Jack can get back on his feet. You'll need to watch everything you say in these next few months. But our day will come. Be patient. I promise you, whoever did this will be at our mercy before this is all over."

"I'm not going to be able to do this without you Bobby. I need you to constantly remember that and help me through all of this. You know I'm not political."

"I know that, Jackie. I'll be there every step of the way," Bobby reassured his brother's wife.

Bobby then embraced his old friend Kenny O'Donnell. As they hugged, O'Donnell whispered in Bobby's ear, "The body in the casket is a guy named Mike Reardon. Jack was admitted to the hospital under Reardon's name." O'Donnell quickly explained how the doctors had admitted Jack into the hospital's intensive care unit under Reardon's name and that people he could absolutely trust were guarding him. With little time and with the cameras of every major network rolling, he told Bobby, "I'll meet you later tonight at your place to give you all the details."

Later that evening O'Donnell drove to Bobby Kelley's home, where they thoroughly planned for Jack's recovery and tried to foresee every possible event that might lead to anyone except a very limited group of insiders knowing of the president's recovery. Kenny carefully thought through each and every event of the day, reconstructed each conversation as best as he could remember it and then recording them on tape. He and Bobby replayed the tape over and over again to be sure they hadn't overlooked anything. It was in the wee hours of Saturday, November 23, when O'Donnell finally headed home to get a few hours of sleep.

The next few weeks and months would be hectic, with the state funeral, the continuing secrecy surrounding Jack's recovery, and, when Jack recovered, going public with the truth of his attempted murder.

Eight months later, looking back over all these extraordinary events, Bobby was convinced he had covered all the bases. He had just called ahead to finalize arrangements for his now-recovered brother to make a nationally televised address to the nation, from WGST in Atlanta. Bobby sat back in his seat, his mind racing from one thought to another as he tried to think of anything he might have overlooked. He had about thirty-five minutes before touchdown at the Atlanta Hartsfield Airport. President Kelley, who had been recuperating at an estate just north of Atlanta, was only an hour or so away from exposing the conspiracy behind his attempted assassination.

The past eight months had been filled with anxiety and anticipation, happiness and disappointment. But for the grace of God and some very talented physicians, Bobby had almost lost his brother. Staring off into the endless horizon at twenty-five thousand feet, he began to reflect upon all the treacherous revelations that he uncovered as he and his team of investigators had secretly assembled the facts surrounding the assassination attempt.

CHAPTER 4

▼

THE COVER-UP BEGINS

Bobby Kelley remembered that bleak night when Air Force One touched down in Washington and he saw his sister-in-law's dress still covered in his brother's blood. He remembered that he found out at the last minute that they were taking the body directly from the plane to Bethesda Naval Hospital to perform an autopsy. It was an executive order approved by the now President Jones. He shuddered to think that Reardon's body was on its way to be autopsied with everyone thinking it was Jack.

"My God, what have I created?" Bobby had thought. "Whoever was behind the assassination attempt would kill anyone to cover up those behind this." They were lucky the whole thing didn't get blown wide open, with the press and everyone else demanding to know who the corpse in the coffin was and where the president's body was. At the time Bobby had no idea that those responsible for the assassination had prearranged to tamper with the body in an attempt to conceal the truth of the killing. It was several weeks later when, in conversation with a friend who had been present at the autopsy, Bobby pieced together what happened that evening of November 22.

Kelley's investigators knew that Kenny O'Donnell was with Dr. Clark when Reardon's body was wrapped in white linen sheets and placed in an expensive viewing coffin before leaving Dallas. When the body arrived at Bethesda for the autopsy, it was in a military body bag placed in a plain wooden casket. When the autopsy began, it was discovered that the president's brain had been removed.

What military officials didn't tell anyone, but what Bobby learned from his own friendly connections, was that before the body went to Bethesda, it was taken to Walter Reed Army Hospital, where a pre-selected team of forensic doctors removed the brain. These Army doctors had to have known it was President Kelley. Why they removed the brain was obvious. Conducting tests on the brain during an official autopsy would have conclusively proved the direction the bullets came from.

Within hours of the shooting, the assassins and their co-conspirators had started to weave their plan to pin the assassination on a lone shooter. Even before the plane carrying what they thought was the president's body arrived in Washington, the FBI and Dallas police had arrested a man and announced that they had caught the president's killer. The suspect was Leonard Osborn, an ex-Marine who had been awarded sharpshooter status during his service years. He had moved to Russia at the height of the tensions between the United States and Russia, just before the Soviet Union dissolved into smaller countries. Dissatisfied with life in Russia, he moved back to the United States and attempted to involve himself in FBI and CIA intelligence. The DIA and CIA knew early on that he would make the perfect patsy.

Under order from President Jones, the military arranged for an autopsy of the president's body. One question Bobby asked himself over and over was who could have ordered a forensic team of doctors at Walter Reed Army Hospital to remove the brain of the president even before it went to Bethesda for the official autopsy? Only a general or admirals could have ordered such an event. The lead forensic scientist at Bethesda Naval Hospital was Commander Holmes, a Medical Naval Officer who had never previously performed an autopsy but who was ordered by his superiors to perform one on the body of the president.

Present at the autopsy were several shadowy characters who identified themselves as CIA and FBI agents. They made a meticulous record of the twenty-five people there that night, and spoke into tape recorders to make notes of each procedure. Before the president's brain was removed, they took photographs of the head wounds, which they then doctored to be consistent with their predetermined findings that a lone assassin shooting from above and behind the president inflicted the wounds.

Perhaps because the military officers had ordered a medical officer who was inexperienced at forensic medicine to conduct the autopsy, they never suspected the body was anyone but the president. None of the doctors, scientists, intelligence officers, or politicians ever questioned that it actually was the President at the procedure. The body before them was of a man who had died from a serious head trauma. The forensic team had no prior knowledge of exactly what kind of wound the president had suffered. They only knew it was a serious head wound. He was about the same age, weight and height as the President, he had the Presidents' chestnut colored hair although seriously distorted and matted by the enormous amount of blood caked within it. There was nothing about the man to raise suspicion. He had the same blood type as the president, and given the enormous swelling of his face, who could have questioned the subtle, minor differences in facial features? The several intelligence agents and military officers who were part of the cover up were so secure in their command of these events, which they must have planned and agonized over for weeks before the assassination, that they simply never let it enter their minds that the body before them could be anyone but the president.

Within days of the assassination, after coming face to face with many facts that all pointed to a cover up, Bobby decided to conduct his own investigation into the assassination and to give his investigative team a code name. He chose the name the Antonio group. This was a group of men loyal to the president that Bobby had charged with assembling evidence surrounding the assassination. Some of the reasons for the early creation of the group was their conclusion: there was major doctoring of photographs taken at the autopsy; the removal of the president's brain was a serious breach of investigative forensic medicine; and records of key parts of the autopsy were altered and doctored to cover up conclusive evidence that the president's wounds were inflicted by more than one shooter. There was now proof positive the assassination was done with the express knowledge of, and perhaps the active participation of, key figures in the Defense Department. If they were not involved in some way, why would they have the president's brain removed before the official autopsy? Why would senior officers order a relative novice to perform the autopsy?

Why, just weeks before the assassination, with the final go ahead for the November 22nd Dallas trip being cleared by the White House on November 4th, did senior officers of the Joint Chiefs order the top three intelligence officers at the DIA to take a month off? Perhaps they were nervous the officers might discover something regarding the assassination that was out of the ordinary. When one of the officers refused, he was permanently reassigned to a less important deck job on the West Coast. When the remaining junior officers saw their new commanding officers hand picked by four-star generals, being concerned about their own careers they quickly fell in line. At the very least these military officers conspired to cover up the identity of others involved, which made them part of the coup d'e.tat.

Bobby later learned from the few close friends the Kelleys had at the Pentagon why the half dozen highly qualified forensic naval doctors present as observers at the autopsy, doctors that between them had performed hundreds of autopsies, had allowed an inexperienced officer who had never performed an autopsy to perform the autopsy on the president. This would allow them cover should any questions about the methods and procedures used during the autopsy ever be questioned. They could deny any knowledge of the events. They could claim they were simply observers.

As mentioned, in attendance at the autopsy were three FBI special agents making very detailed notes of who was present and what everyone said and did. Those notes included the lead forensic doctors' procedures, the photographs of those in attendance and all comments made by them. The notes were turned over to the FBI Director Jay E. Howard and never made available to the Attorney General, who just happened to be the president's brother and the FBI Director's boss. The records of the autopsy promptly disappeared.

Bobby also later learned that Vice President Jones, now President Jones, after being sworn in on Air Force One as it sat at the Dallas airport less than one hour after the bullets rang out, received numerous telephone calls after arriving back at the White House that evening. Five of the calls were from FBI Director Howard. In a highly unusual move, a number of the president's regular Secret Service detail had taken vacation time that week and were replaced by other agents. The newly sworn-in President Jones also placed calls to key political leaders asking them to be part of a committee to investigate the president's murder. These were carefully selected government officials who would never have been permitted under U.S. law to serve on a jury at the trial of Osborn, the accused assassin. Yet they actually did serve as jurors, handpicked by President Jones to form a commission that accepted testimony from witnesses against Osborn, without Osborn having the benefit of an advocate (a lawyer representing Osborn's interests) to cross-examine that testimony. This was in effect a murder trial against a United States citizen in which he was denied his constitutional right to a fair trial, with the chairman of the commission being the Chief Justice of the Supreme Court. Four of the 6 "jurors" were senators and congressmen.

From his arrest, Osborn requested an attorney but was never allowed to speak to one. Seasoned FBI agents, who incidentally were attorneys, questioned him for hours on end and by veteran District Attorneys and high-ranking police officials who all knew they had denied Osborn's constitutional right to have an attorney present during questioning. They knew that any information obtained during such questioning was inadmissible, yet they continued. The questioning went on into the night with the police parading Osborn in front of the TV cameras on two occasions. Each time he publicly professed his innocence and claimed that he was set up as a patsy. Could they have already known there would never be an Osborn trial after the events of Sunday two days from then?

Not only were Osborn's constitutional rights denied while he was alive now, several months after his murder, the accused assassin's rights to a fair trial were being trampled upon once again by the committee of government officials hand-picked to investigate the president's murder. These officials had taken an oath to uphold the Constitution of the United States. Now, under that oath, the testimony they were listening to was top secret; they had closed their committee hearings to the public. Several members of the commission, including a very high-ranking Senator from Georgia, complained that he was never notified when or where the committee hearings would take place, despite the fact that he frequently requested such knowledge. This sham of a committee investigating the murder of a President of the United States would become known as the Werner Commission.

All of Robert Kelley's enemies were almost gleefully confident that he had lost all his power; now that the president was dead, he was a lame duck Attorney General with little or no clout. There was no hint of the fact that Jack was still alive. A small team of loyal Secret Service Agents, some of whom had been told by their superiors to take some vacation time prior to the Dallas trip, were guarding him. Hearing of the assassination they had rushed to contact other members of their trusted inner core, and were carefully screened before being allowed to join with the president's regular Secret Service detail in guarding Jack.

These members of the president's elite Secret Service detail were embarrassed to learn of the number of changes their superiors and those who filled in for them had made to the president's original trip plans. They knew these changes were highly unusual, impromptu field changes that should never have been permitted. From the moments the shots were fired, having questioned the changes made in the field, they knew it was a setup. Now the least they could do was guard their president from any further harm, and keep their mouths shut about it until someone could sort everything out and get to the bottom of who was responsible.

No one was even mildly suspicious when the agents guarding the president gave as their excuse for their sudden vacation requests their need "to emotionally sort things out after the assassination." Anxious to have the president's Secret Service Detail temporarily incommunicado, the FBI was quick and generous when granting their time-off requests. The agents would spend time guarding the wounded president until the truth unfolded and the president's people could relieve them. They were accustomed to working closely with Kenny O'Donnell, Dave Powers, Bobby Kelley, and the president's group. They didn't always agree with their politics, but they trusted them and liked them.

Just hours after the assassination, the conspirators, emboldened by the apparently successful murder of the president of the United States, framed some poor slob to look like he was the lone assassin. In the excitement of the announcement that they had arrested the man they accused of killing the president, no one picked up on the fact that the Dallas police had broadcast a description of Osborn twelve minutes after the president was shot. The broadcast was in connection with the shooting death of a Dallas police officer named Tibbitt. The police broadcast occurred at 12:43 PM on November 22. Officer Tibbitt was not shot until 1:06 PM.

Officer Tibbitt was murdered by a man who had started talking to him as the officer stopped him. Tibbitt was shot when he got out of his police car. Helen Marksman was the only eyewitness to the Tibbitt shooting. As the man who shot the police officer made his getaway, he ran right up to Ms. Marksman with the gun still in his hand. Ms. Marksman later described to reporters the police affidavit she had signed, in which she described the shooter as a "young white man, short and a little heavy, with somewhat bushy hair." The broadcast played by the Dallas police twenty-three minutes before Tibbitt was shot had described Osborn as follows: "He was of average height or a little taller, slim with receding hair." The police affidavit's only description of Osborn was that he was a "young white man." Bobby's Antonio investigators were baffled as to why, in this very early unfolding of events, the Dallas police would omit the actual description and change the one given by Ms. Marksman? And why would the police suggest the murder of Officer Tibbitt was somehow tied to the assassination, and change the description of the only eyewitness to the Tibbitt murder to fit the description of the man they wanted to accuse of the president's assassination?

Ms. Markham's affidavit formed the entire case against Osborn in the murder of Officer Tibbitt, but at a news conference that November 22 afternoon, Dallas District Attorney Thomas Wade asserted, "We have more evidence to prove Osborn killed Tibbitt than we have to show he killed the president."

Two days after the assassination of the president, despite the fact that security should have been at an extremely tight level, a small-time Mob operative known to just about every Dallas police officer walked up to Osborn while FBI agents were transferring him to a more secure location and shot him with a .38 caliber pistol. The Mob operative did so in front of the whole world, with the TV cameras rolling. The accused assassin would never be able to tell his story, to share his claim that he was being framed and "was a patsy." Osborn had made this claim from the time he was arrested. The Antonio investigators concluded that perhaps it was no coincidence, given all the "accommodative moves" by Dallas police that the Dallas police chief had been in the car with Vice President Jones as he drove from the hospital back to Air Force One the day of the assassination.

President John Francis Kelley (in the person of Mike Reardon) had been laid to rest after the pomp and ceremony of a state funeral attended by dozens of heads of state. President Jones moved to solidify his power, naming a high-level commission to investigate the assassination. Arriving at the White House at about 6:45 PM, about the same time Jack Kelley's body was arriving at Bethesda for its autopsy, President Jones spoke with several past presidents in successive five-and ten-minute phone calls. While eating dinner he met with a congressional delegation.

In what must have been a well-thought-out plan, the evening of November 22, Jones called at least four members of the soon-to-be-named Werner Commission and got them to agree to serve. It would be the only government body to ever investigate the murder of the president. Jones purposely included two members from the House, two members from the Senate, a member of the intelligence community in the person of former CIA Director Allen Dunlap, a representative of the big-money people in the person of the president of the World Bank, and a member of the Judiciary in the person of the Chief Justice of the Supreme Court. With this group in place, he would thwart any congressional attempt to have independent public hearings, and retain control of the final findings. Several senators and congressmen continued to publicly call for congressional hearings on the assassination, but President Jones invited them to meet with him in the White House, and they quickly fell in line. No congressional hearings were ever held.

Upon learning who the members of the investigative commission would be, Bobby became certain that the conspirators were confident they had pulled off their coup d'etat, and he could function without anyone being suspect of him. In fact, having witnessed Jack's tear-jerking funeral service, with all its pomp and ceremony, several of Bobby's lifelong enemies now actually felt sorry for him and his family.

For several weeks after the funeral, about every eight or ten days Bobby received an envelope at his office in the Justice Department. There was no return address, but the envelope was postmarked Alexandria, Virginia, a city just over the state line, a suburb of Washington, DC. The sender used postage stamps, not a traceable postage meter. At first the contents were simple typed notes expressing the author's regret at the loss of the president, one of the thousands of letters received by the Kelley family. Then one of the notes expressed the sender's regret that he was unable to prevent what had happened. This got Bobby's attention, "who could this be that he might have been able to prevent the assassination." The latest note stated that he would continue to send information about those who conspired to kill the president. There was no way of telling where these notes were coming from, and so far, aside from the comments about being able to prevent the assassination and possibly knowing who the conspirators were, the writer had revealed nothing particularly earth shattering.

Bobby met Sean McDonald at 10 PM Thursday at a local pancake house. The two men embraced.

"I'm so sorry, Bobby," Sean said. "Jack was a very special friend, and I know how close you guys were. I can't find the words to express what a deep sense of loss I feel. I can't even imagine how your family is coping."

"Sean, you know I consider you a close friend. That's why I asked if you could help me and my family through this tragedy," Bobby replied.

The men sat down and ordered coffee and discussed the events surrounding the assassination. In the years since they attended Harvard, Bobby had asked Sean to be godfather to one of his kids. Sean reciprocated and asked Bobby to be godfather for his firstborn son. They had been in each other's wedding parties, and Sean's wife Susan and Bobby's wife Nancy had been sorority sisters. They had gone through college together and had kept in touch through the years.

Early in the conversation, Bobby leaned closer to Sean and in a quiet whisper said, "Sean I need to confide in you. What I am about to tell you is an incredible story that you must swear you will not repeat to anyone."

"Bobby, what's wrong? You sound so serious. You know I would never betray your trust."

"Sean, Jack's not dead! It will be several weeks and maybe months before he's out of the woods, then several more months for Jack to recuperate enough to face the task of confronting his enemies. How all this would play out for Jack, I'm not exactly sure at this point But for now we're just taking it one step at a time."

"That's fantastic, it's amazing, how did you ever pull this off Bobby"? "Do you know who was behind the shooting"? Sean was elated at the news that the president was still alive. "What can I do to help?" he asked.

"The important thing now is to give Jack time to mend," Bobby said. "The finger pointing, accusations, and reprisals will come later, when he's back on his feet again. What I do know, even at this early stage, is that there was involvement by high-ranking government officials, Pentagon intelligence, generals and admirals, FBI, and the Secret Service. I believe a Mafia hit squad and even have reason to suspect that President Jones had a hand in it. So we're up against some formidable enemies. This could be some very serious duty you're volunteering for."

"You've known me for over twenty years, Bobby. When have I ever backed down from a challenge?" Sean shot back.

Knowing these guys would not hesitate to kill again, and with some reckless abandon Bobby changed the subject a little, pointing out to Sean how it was natural to kill your enemies in time of war. Bobby needed to know Sean's attitude about some of the things he was about to discuss, so he was careful in choosing his words. He needed to know Sean's attitude about preemptive strikes against this group of presidential conspirators. Perhaps they would even need to murder some of them.

"Sean, while this might not be a typical war, we could find ourselves in a war-like environment where we are forced to kill preemptively. How do you feel about killing some of those people who struck at our president, the head of our constitutional form of government, and in effect took over our government by allowing their man to assume leadership? How would you feel about the elimination of some of these conspirators? Would your Special Forces units have any problem following orders if those orders involved the murder of civilians, generals, and high-ranking politicians?"

Sean thought for about three seconds before saying, "As an officer in the United States Marines, I took an oath to uphold our constitution. As far as I'm concerned, my commander in chief is the duly appointed head of the military. But my commander in chief also happens to be my lifelong friend, so my allegiance is to the president."

Bobby then asked if he could absolutely trust the Special Forces unit that Sean commanded. Sean said he spent a lot of time with these men and had even risked his life with them. As a team of twelve, they had been the third team sent behind enemy lines in Afghanistan several weeks before the war started. Sean knew from having spent weeks alone with each of these men that they were totally committed to their country and supported the president both politically and militarily.

"Bobby let me assure you, I know these guys. They will be committed to Jack's well-being. Even though they don't know him personally, he's their commander in chief."

"I believe those responsible for this were trying to overthrow our duly elected government," Sean went on. "They have to be eliminated, and treated as if they were an invading army. I offer you my services, whatever you and the president need of me. My unit will stand at our Commander in Chief's side and defend him against any further attacks."

"Even if it meant preemptive strikes to take out those spies who were undermining our mission in saving our very form of government?" Bobby asked.

Sean quickly responded "Bobby, I'm offering to have the men in my unit, men whom I would trust with my life, available under top-secret conditions to do whatever the president asks of us."

Bobby and Sean then discussed the immediate problem of how to secure the safety of the recuperating president and relieve the Secret Service detail who were on twelve-hour shifts guarding his room. It was now almost a week after the shooting, and here were four absolutely devoted Secret Servicemen taking turns being with the president. It was a dangerous and exhausting job. No one knew for sure that those people responsible for the attempted murder wouldn't walk through the door at any moment and kill both them and the president.

Bobby asked Sean to speak, confidentially, with his Special Forces unit, and to put together a plan to ensure the president would have twenty-four-hour protection. Sean would have to put together a schedule of who would cover the President and when and they couldn't do that without the express commitment of the entire unit. Several of Sean's men were family men, and this commitment would take sacrifice. They would have to be apart from their families, and they could not confide to their spouses the nature of their mission. If the conspirators got any inkling that the president was alive, they would do whatever it took to finish the job. Endangering innocent family members of the men protecting the president would certainly be part of any possible scenario. This was a mission that required absolute secrecy.

Bobby told Sean that even if the conspirators had to blow up the entire hospital, killing hundreds of innocent people, they would do it, and they would make it look like some sort of accident. Understanding the graveness of the problems they faced, Bobby and Sean shook hands. Bobby told Sean he would be in touch in the next thirty-six hours.

The logistics of setting up transportation for members of the special presidential guard had to be well planned. Nothing could stand out as unusual, or someone might start asking questions and blow the cover off the entire project. Bobby had previously decided on the code name the "Antonio Group." Being a student of history, he had always admired the Roman general Marc Antony. Although he was just a few yards away from him at the time, Antony was unable to save his best friend, Caesar, from being assassinated by members of the Roman Senate. Antony publicly vowed revenge. Within four days he had murdered over three hundred people he suspected of being involved in either the actual execution or in its planning. Among the dead were Senators, judges, and wealthy Patricians. In some cases whole families were slaughtered. Within nine months of Caesar's assassination, Antony had killed over 3,400 people he suspected were complicit in Caesar's murder.

Bobby's anger ran deep. He would have to bide his time, but he would get even with those responsible for trying to kill his brother. He didn't think the Antonio group would be easy for his enemies to detect. He would rent a small office in the huge Watergate Building and install a phone there so that the members of the group would have a central place to meet and leave coded telephone messages. Bobby even opened an Antonio Club checking account at a local bank and deposited $50,000 to cover the expenses associated with his brother's recovery and the security costs of guarding him.

The club's board of directors would number twelve. Four would represent Sean's unit of presidential guardians and be his military command. Another four would represent the inner circle of the president's trusted Secret Service detail. With their inside knowledge of White House and Secret Service procedures, they would interface with the military members. The remaining four would be the investigative team whose job it would be to independently investigate anything and everything to do with events relative to the assassination.

Each of the twelve would be known only by his first name. Under no circumstances would members of the group ever e-mail one another with sensitive messages. They were to meet, at the club's offices, only when a meeting was absolutely necessary. Bobby would arrange to have the phone and office "swept" every few days to ensure that no one bugged the place. All material retrieved during the investigation of facts relative to the assassination would be reviewed weekly by Bobby, O'Donnell, O'Brien, and Powell. Each would have the capability to retrieve messages from the club's phone.

The Kelley family owned two Learjets which various members of the family had access to when they couldn't or didn't want to fly on a commercial airline. Bobby contacted five key members of his family to discuss the use of the jets. Without going into great detail, he explained that for the next several months he would need to have exclusive use of both jets, or that at the very least they would have to give seventy-two hours notice before using the transportation. He explained that it was of the utmost importance that they not say a word about his need for the jets to anyone, even other family members. If asked, they should say that the jets were being serviced or were on a tight schedule of use. He further instructed that he should be informed immediately of any such inquiry.

"For now I need your absolute trust," he said to the family members he called. "You'll understand everything later."

Three of Sean's Special Forces members were rated to fly Learjets, as was one of the four Secret Service men. That gave Bobby four pilots he could trust as well. There was also a longtime family employee and pilot Bobby could count on. Bobby didn't make this man privy to what was going on, but he had flown hundreds of political missions for the Kelley family and knew not to ask any questions or divulge any details about the comings and goings of the family jets.

CHAPTER 5

▼

SILENCING THE PATSY

In Dallas, two days after the president was killed, the FBI was transporting the alleged assassin to another jail. Leonard Osborn was a former U.S. Marine. He received an honorable discharge from service in 1986, but the authorities revoked it, giving him a dishonorable discharge, months later, after he moved to Russia. Osborn married a Russian girl, and just before the 1992 breakup of the Soviet Union moved back to the United States.

Bobby knew that under normal conditions, the transporting of a suspect in such a high-profile case would have been done in complete secrecy, with heavily armed security. Not in Osborn's case. In a highly unusual move, the government announced to the national press that they would move the president's accused killer to "a more secure jail" at 11 AM on Sunday, November 24. The move quickly became a media event. A dozen or so television cameras were trained on the alleged assassin as Dallas police detectives escorted Osborn through an underground garage from the jail to a vehicle waiting to transport Osborn to a more secure environment. A crowd had gathered to watch the event, though evidently this didn't concern the authorities—aside from the presence of a small number of Dallas police officers, security was almost nonexistent. When suddenly a man stepped out of the crowd with a pistol in his hand, took two or three steps and shot the alleged presidential assassin in the stomach, missing his heart by little more than an inch. Osborn was rushed to a hospital and lived about an hour before dying from his injuries.

Jack Sarubi, the man who shot Osborn, was well-known to the Dallas police force. He had been a small-time Mob operative living in Chicago before he moved to Dallas to help his sister run a local bar. It wasn't long before he sought the blessing and protection of the local Mafia boss and changed the bar into a strip joint.

Sarubi had met earlier that Sunday morning in his apartment with his attorney and three reporters. All four men would be murdered within months of that meeting. Every Dallas police officer was familiar with Sarubi. Two days prior, Sarubi was at the Parkland Hospital when the president was rushed into the emergency room. He was already there when the president's limo arrived. Was this a coincidence? The Kelley investigative team doubted it.

How, Bobby wondered, did Sarubi get to be standing with a pistol in his hand within a few feet of the route Osborn would take? How was it possible that a well-known local Mob guy could walk up to a suspected presidential assassin and shoot him dead? How was it that the area was not properly secured? Why wasn't security around Osborn incredibly tight?

Bobby could see how someone could be inclined to blame the Dallas police department, but at the time of Osborn's move the FBI, CIA, and Secret Service were still actively continuing their questioning of him, so they were very much involved in planning the Osborn transfer to safer quarters. In fact, the "jail" Osborn was being moved to was in the FBI building. Then there was the fact that the president's Secret Service detail, those responsible for the president's safety, were out until 3:30 AM in Jack Sarubi's bar the night before the president was shot? Was this just another coincidence? The Antonio group's investigators were piecing together a string of such "coincidences," looking for the connections that joined them. In this case the Mob connection was unmistakable.

The Antonio group's investigative arm was already collecting information ten days after the shooting. These were a small group of trusted staff members who had been with the Kelleys during their rise to political power. They were criminal attorneys and investigative assistants trained in the assembly of facts for presenting in a court of law. The group learned that those responsible for the presidents' assassination attempt probably would have killed Osborn sooner had he not been captured so quickly and taken immediately to the Dallas police headquarters. Killing the "lone assassin" would silence everyone.

Few people took note that the man who silenced Osborn was originally from Chicago, that he had a past speckled with run-ins with the law, and that he had been arrested several times for minor criminal activity. Sarubi made no effort to hide his association with both Dallas and Chicago Mob figures. In fact, he boasted of those connections. Noteworthy was the fact that Sam Giacondo, the Chicago Mafia boss who helped elect Jack Kelley through his deal to swing union votes, had numerous dealings with the Mafia capo that ran Dallas. Antonio investigators knew this was anything but coincidence.

Upon learning the details of Osborn's murder, Bobby Kelley realized how superbly orchestrated the killing was. Captured less than two hours after the assassination and a few hours before the nightly news programs, Osborn was painted as the lone assassin from the very beginning. In fact, no one ever questioned that there could have been others involved. Film taken during Osborn's interrogation in the Dallas police headquarters showed him denying he had anything to do with the president's shooting. He claimed he was framed and set up as a patsy. Further film footage showed detectives displaying the rifle they said was used in the shooting of the president. All of this information was made public by the Dallas police department, with the FBI directing the release to the news media of each part of the story. Nothing about the assassination was released in Dallas without the approval of government authorities in Washington.

The Antonio investigators knew that Dallas Police officials performed paraffin tests on Osborn almost immediately upon his arrest. When a person fires a gun, tiny particles of gunpowder are expelled from the gun. These particles create a residue that is difficult to wash off and can easily be detected. Although Osborn was charged with the shooting death of a Dallas police officer, the paraffin test showed that he had not fired a gun. If Osborn had not known anything about the shooting, he would simply have claimed he was innocent, but at every opportunity he claimed that he was "set up and being made a patsy." Would Osborn's testimony have implicated those he thought were setting him up? Would the public naming of those individuals Osborn claimed were setting him up have pointed a finger at some of the conspirators? Hours passed and the questioning of Osborn continued. Despite his frequent requests for an attorney, Osborn was denied his constitutional rights and was not allowed to speak with a lawyer until the next day. His interrogators were highly experienced, seasoned attorneys, police officers, and FBI agents (some of whom were also attorneys). Why would these men jeopardize such a high-profile national case by denying Osborn his right to have an attorney present? They all knew that any evidence obtained during such questioning was inadmissible. Why would they continue questioning Osborn for hours unless they already knew that there would never be a trial?

Politically ambitious District Attorney Wade called a news conference knowing full well that he would be speaking to a national audience. He announced that Osborn had taken a bus after he shot the president, and had then been picked up seven blocks away from the crime scene by a cab driver named Daryl Click. DA Wade claimed that Mr. Click signed an affidavit to that effect. He also claimed that Click worked for the City Transportation Company. Upon further investigation it was learned that "Daryl Click" had not only never worked for the City Transportation Company, but that he did not exist. When confronted with that information, DA Wade stated that the cab driver's name was actually William Whaley. But Whaley's logbook shows he picked Osborn up at 12:30. The president was shot at 12:31. Why would these basic facts not jibe? How could Osborn travel on a bus for seven blocks and then have a cab driver show he was picked up before the shots were fired? Why would District Attorney Wade provide the name of someone who did not exist?

Summarizing the official story released by coordinated agencies of the FBI, CIA, Secret Service and the Dallas police, Osborn shot the president, got on a city bus to escape the crime scene, traveled seven blocks in city traffic (perhaps ten to fifteen minutes) where a presidential visit had jammed the flow of normal traffic, exited the city bus and hailed a cab to complete his get away.

The media was given detailed information about this obscure ex-Marine sharpshooter immediately after he was arrested, but it should have taken a day or so to uncover this data. The details of Osborn's life weren't pretty. When he was a youth his family moved more than fifteen times in as many years. Psychologists presented by the authorities claimed that moving a child fifteen times from one city to another would disrupt the child's development. The child would not develop normal relationships with other schoolchildren because he would always be the new guy on the block. His education would also suffer; subject matter would be different in each school.

Osborn joined the Marines, where he learned to speak fluent Russian. When he was honorably discharged a few years later he "defected" to Russia, where he showed up one day at the U.S. Embassy and, according to official U.S. documents, "tried" to denounce his U.S. citizenship. Despite having no personal wealth or source of income, in the two and a half years he lived in Russia he received a monthly check from an anonymous source that proved to be untraceable. When he returned to the United States, he joined several radical groups and was painted as a disturbed, secretive Russian KGB operative.

Photographs of Osborn showing his welted face and swollen eyes made it obvious he had been beaten by the police during his arrest. It was all so seamless. They got their man! Those insiders who knew what was going on now had their warning: toe the line, be quiet and do your part in the cover-up, or die. We got the President we can get you!

Osborn had always been interested in, if not infatuated with, the idea of working undercover for the CIA. The CIA played on that by inviting him to several meetings where they set him up to think he was going to infiltrate a "Saudi group of Islamists" and then report back on their activities. Incredibly, he somehow could not see past the obvious fact that with his fair complexion he stood out like a sore thumb against the darker-skinned men. He had an ash white complexion and simply would never blend in with a group of men with darker complexion and black hair. But the CIA convinced him that the "Islamists" would find him useful for gaining access to areas marked for terrorist attacks that they would have trouble gaining access to due to their ethnic appearances. To Osborn this seemed reasonable, given the recent attacks on the World Trade Center and Pentagon. Osborn thought he had finally achieved his goal of working for the CIA.

In reality Osborn was being set up to take the fall for the assassination. The group of "Islamists" were in fact Arab CIA agents acting as terrorists. When the Antonio Group pieced together all these facts they realized that even the CIA agents masquerading as Islamist terrorists were uninformed parts of the deception created by those senior intelligence officers who were part of the real plot against the President. This "Saudi Islamic cell" was boldly making plans to assassinate the president of the United States. An alarmed Osborn dutifully reported to CIA operatives what the terrorists were planning. Insiders at the CIA knew they had the man who would take the fall for the real assassination being planned later that year.

CHAPTER 6

▼

STILL PRESUMED DEAD

Bobby couldn't believe it—the president's funeral was absolutely magnificently staged. Jackie had planned the thing to a T. The job had been emotionally upsetting for her, though. With each decision she made she had to ward off tears, thinking how she could have been planning the real thing. She consulted with Bobby on just about everything but in the final analysis she basically made all the decisions. She had always been a happy, upbeat person, but now, having to plan the details of her husband's funeral, even though it was in reality a mock funeral, she seemed to be slipping in and out of depression. This was truly a difficult time for the first lady.

Jackie had arranged to have the president's closed casket lay in state under the Capitol Dome, in the same spot where the assassinated body of President Lincoln had rested 138 years before. Ordinary people lined up for several miles to pay their respects. They stood in line for hours, winding in and out of the police barricades set up to control the crowds, to spend no more than ten or fifteen seconds in front of the casket. World leaders arrived the day before the President was to be laid to rest and held meetings with the new president. President Kelley had served in the Navy and was a military hero. He was given a full-blown military funeral, with a 21-gun salute, fighter plane flyover, military bands, the whole nine yards."

"Under the circumstances," Bobby jokingly commented to O'Brien during the service, "those of us who know this is a charade should get an Oscar." Bobby hoped all the foreign dignitaries would forgive them once they learned the truth that Jack wasn't really dead. The cameras were on Bobby constantly, and he had to hold back a smile several times while standing alongside Jackie at the grave. "Poor Jack," Bobby thought, "when it's really his time, will anyone actually believe it and come to his funeral?" Jack's real funeral might be the only funeral for a former president of the United States attended by only his family. Months after the funeral Jack viewed film of the event and was probably the first person in history to critique his own funeral.

Jackie was the picture of etiquette. She was eventually going to have to move out of the White House, as Jack would never recover before the new president wanted to occupy the White House. She would move back into the town home they purchased when Jack was elected to the Senate. But she was handling it extremely well, and while she was longing to visit her husband and be with him while he convalesced, she knew that for now that would be impossible. For the next few months or more she would have to be content with verbal reports from her husband's brother and trusted friends updating her on how he was progressing.

Jackie longed for the day she could put her arms around her husband once more, she missed him so much. The day before the shooting she had told Jack that she really didn't want to go on this trip, she all but despised political events, but Jack convinced her that he needed her at his side. She was so glad she was there with him when he needed her most. She would never forget the look he gave her as their eyes met in the split second after the first bullet struck. He knew he was in trouble. It was a look of good-bye! The look continued to haunt her, darkening her thoughts. She would never forget it. Each time it popped into her mind her whole personality changed.

On the day of the shooting, consultation between O'Donnell, Doctor Clark and the rest of the medical team determined that it would not be wise to attempt to move Jack, he was simply to close to death to risk moving him anywhere. Yet he couldn't stay in the emergency room, people are treated in the ER and either released or admitted to the hospital for further treatment. So Doctor Clark admitted the president to the hospital as one of his patients under the name of Mike Reardon. They didn't know if anyone would come looking for Reardon but they had few options so they took a chance. In intensive care the president could be closely monitored and the doctors could respond quickly with whatever care he required. The intensive care unit offered one other important feature, it was a smaller area and more easily defended against assault should it ever come to that.

The team of doctors and nurses who cared for the president after he was admitted to the intensive care unit responded with an incredible sense of patriotism. They made trips to the hospital on their own time just to make sure everything was OK, bumping into one another when their visits overlapped. Between the normal care any intensive care patient would receive from the on-duty nurses, and the ten original members of the president's emergency room team, the president was attended to twenty-four hours a day, seven days a week. None of the hospital officials had any suspicions about the patient named Mike Reardon. Bobby had arranged to pay the hospital weekly through one of his family's corporations.

As long as the bills were paid promptly, they never wondered about patients' identities. Decades before Bobby's grandfather had set up several "dummy" corporate structures during prohibition to conduct business in the import of Scotch, a business he didn't want the public to know he was part of. Over the 60 or so years since the partners in those corporate structures were made to appear as the only stockholders, leaving the Kelley name off any association with those corporate structures, although the Kelley family still controlled them.

"Mr. Reardon" was still unconscious five days after the assassination attempt. His vital signs were improving, but the shot to his head had left him with a swelling brain. Several times doctors had to relieve brain pressure caused by the fluid buildup the body generates when it is damaged so severely.

The president's neck wound was also troubling. The bleeding had stopped, and the small tear the bullet made in the president's windpipe had been repaired, but he was still struggling to breathe normally and had to be kept on oxygen.

The day after Bobby's meeting with Sean, the two men had agreed to arrange for twenty-four-hour protection for "Mr. Reardon" through Sean's Special Forces unit. Dressed in civilian clothes, the Special Forces members took overlapping eight-hour shifts, with two of them at the president's bedside at any given time. Being their commander and given the frequent clandestine missions these elite soldiers were called upon to perform, Sean could easily cover for his men being absent on a rotating basis.

The doctors were worried that the president might remain in a coma for some time, so they created a story that Mr. Reardon was a wealthy businessman who had had a stroke and required brain surgery. The story would give them the cover they needed to explain to the other medical professionals the security and special medical care that this patient was getting. It also gave them the chance to bandage most of the president's face and conceal his identity.

Eventually Bobby would have to decide where to move his brother when he woke up and began further recovery. The Kelley family was good friends with a wealthy Atlanta businessman who owned a four-hundred-acre farm on the outskirts of Atlanta. Once his brother was well enough to travel, Bobby planned to ask the businessman if "Mr. Reardon" could spend a few weeks at the estate as his guest. Bobby knew his brother would be more than welcome at his friend's estate, but didn't want to chance any leak of his brother's survival before he absolutely had to. Right now he was safe, he had 24 hour protection by men capable of taking out a dozen people before they would get to him, and from the position the special forces people had the President's bed set up within the ward, no one could approach without them being aware. The President's face was so swollen from the traumatic experience, his head so covered with bandages as was his neck, that no one would recognize who he was for the time being.

Exactly one week after the assassination shots were fired, President Jones signed executive order #11130, creating a commission to investigate the assassination. The group was to be known as the Werner Commission, after its chairman, Earl Werner, the Chief Justice of the Supreme Court. Bobby knew immediately that the commission would not get to the bottom of what really happened. It was obvious by the men President Jones had appointed to the commission. He confided to O'Donnell, "These guys will put on a good show, but that's all it will ever turn out to be. They are political hacks. Political drones used to being insiders and accustomed to walking lock step with their cronies in the Washington political scene. The cover-up is in full swing, and LBJ is taking a major role in it."

One of the men President Jones selected for the Werner Commission was Allen Dunlap. President Kelley had fired Dunlap from his position as head of the CIA about sixteen months before the assassination attempt. His selection by President Jones to serve on the Werner commission, and having the chance to turn the other way when incriminating facts pointing to the assassins were presented, would be sweet revenge for Dunlap. Dunlap's political savvy and the underworld contacts he had established while head of the CIA told him that the CIA had to have had a part in the assassination. The last thing Dunlap wanted to do was be part of an investigation that would target his lifelong friends at the CIA. Years of running the CIA had made him callous. Dunlap no longer acted out of patriotic duty, and he was well aware that many thought his hatred for the Kelleys meant he was personally involved in the assassination in one way or another.

Allen's father, John Foster Dunlap, had been the head of the CIA from its inception. Prior to the creation of the Central Intelligence Agency by Congress in

1946 the United States operated its intelligence gathering through an agency known as the OSS. In fact, Allen's dad had been Director of the OSS during World War Two. The senior Dunlap stationed himself in neutral Switzerland during the war and had worked closely with General Eisenhower when Ike was Supreme Commander of Allied Forces. After Ike became president in 1952 Dunlap was appointed CIA Director by Ike. Using tens of millions of dollars at his disposal, Foster Dunlap financed the French, Dutch and Polish resistance and had a long history of working with underworld figures, before, during, and after the World War Two invasion of Italy. In Italy, weeks before the Allies invaded that country, he used the Mafia to kill dozens of German officers, sabotage German munitions depots so they would be short of both leaders and ammunition and generally cause havoc in the German army.

These Mafia capos received millions of dollars and numerous political favors in return. Nothing was more important to the Allies than the defeat of the German military machine and toward that end, no price was too high or favor too large. In one such political deal, for his part in disrupting the German Military before the invasion of Italy, the U.S. government, in addition to paying him millions of dollars, allowed Vito Genevese to reenter the United States. Genevese had been deported to Italy for being convicted of murder in throwing his lovers husband off a five-story building after being discovered as an adulterous, just before the war began.

The United States also allowed Charlie "Lucky" Luciano to be deported to Italy, commuting his jail sentence for prostitution. While he was indicted for several counts of murder, the only crime Thomas Dewey, the New York prosecutor, could convict Luciano of was prostitution and even that charge was clouded by the accusations of witnesses of questionable character. Luciano, who was the undisputed "Capo de Capo," boss of bosses, by 1941 had served about six years of a twenty-year sentence in a maximum-security upstate New York prison. Riding on the wave of national media coverage of the Luciano trial, which got even greater coverage on the east coast, Dewey would later be elected Governor of New York and then go on to be nominated the Republican candidate for president against Democrat Harry Truman in 1948.

Early in 1942, several senior military intelligence officers visited Luciano in prison. They needed his help in stopping the sabotage on U.S. docks of the goods being shipped to Europe to fuel the U.S. war machine. The sabotage was beginning to affect the United States' ability to supply its troops overseas. Luciano and friends controlled the dockworkers unions, so the military intelligence officers made him a deal. When the war was over, they would commute Luciano's prison term and deport him back to Italy where he would live in luxury. In the meantime they would transfer him from the upstate New York maximum-security prison to a minimum-security prison closer to New York City, allow him to have his own chef, and let him have frequent conjugal visits.

The German government under Hitler's guidance from 1933 had trained many of its high school students to speak perfect English, years before its preparation for its war against the west. In fact many were taught to speak different dialects of American English, Southern, New England, etc in order to blend into the general population. The few saboteurs who were caught told of how they swam ashore after German U-boats dropped them and hundreds of others a mile or two offshore. With huge numbers of American males off fighting the war in Europe and the Pacific, getting a job on the docks was easy. It was hard physical work more suited for males rather than females.

Within forty-eight hours of accepting this deal, Luciano was moved to the minimum-security prison. Almost immediately along the East, West, and Gulf Coasts, so many blond-haired, fair-skinned males were found floating in American waters that the sabotage along the docks was all but eliminated over the next ninety days. Even those saboteurs who were inadvertently passed over by Luciano's people knew that to continue to disrupt shipments would eventually expose them and that they would die just as many of their fellow saboteurs had. So they simply went to work every day and became part of American society. These underworld connections cultivated by the senior Dunlap were passed on to the younger Dunlap when he started his CIA career following in his father's footsteps.

Some sixteen months before the assassination, in the days leading up to the invasion of Afghanistan, Allen Dunlap was squarely on the side of those Pentagon officials who were plotting against President Kelley's proposed military changes. Dunlap began to quietly instruct his CIA operatives within Afghanistan to bribe Taliban officials and discreetly leak details of the upcoming invasion to them. With hundreds of billions of dollars of Pentagon budget funds at stake, Dunlap wanted to make sure that President Kelley failed in his effort to rid Afghanistan of the Taliban. It wasn't that Dunlap thought the Taliban should stay; it was rather that the invasion of Afghanistan would be the first testing of the new, fast track, and lightweight military. Moreover, the whole thing was being done without the support of the senior military officers Dunlap had agreed and sympathized with. It was in Dunlap's and the CIA's interests to keep the status quo, and that meant standing against the changes this new president wanted to implement.

The political genius of Jones' appointment of Dunlap to be a member of the Werner Commission was that he knew, without even having a conversation with Dunlap about it, exactly how Dunlap would respond to evidence that pointed to CIA or DIA involvement in the conspiracy.

In fact, therein laid the political genius of the appointment of each of the Werner Commission's members. The assassination behind them, President Kelley presumed by all to be dead, the cover up in full swing, President Jones was displaying his considerable powers of persuasion as he went about consolidating his power base.

CHAPTER 7

▼

THE SLEEPING GIANT
STRIKES BACK

On September 11, 2001 without any discernable warning, in an act of war directed toward the United States and all it stood for, members of a terrorist group known as Al Quada hijacked four commercial U.S. airplanes. Two of the airliners were flying out of Boston. Armed with box cutters they had concealed from inspectors, the terrorists flew these two planes into the World Trade Center. With fuel tanks filled to capacity both of these planes were destined for California. The hijackers, who had previously taken flying lessons, aimed the fuel-laden aircraft into the middle of the buildings, trapping thousands on the floors above the impact. Little more than one hour after being struck by the first plane, the South tower of the World Trade Center collapsed. Minutes later the North tower fell. Never before had commercial airplanes been used as missiles. Never before had foreigners so boldly attacked the U.S. homeland.

Another of the other hijacked planes, this one departing from Washington, flew into the Pentagon, killing several hundred military personnel, generals and civilian office workers among them. The fourth plane crashed in a field in Pennsylvania after turning off its original western course and heading southeast, back toward Washington. Many of the passengers on board that flight had received calls on their cell phones from loved ones checking on their safety.

During those phone calls, passengers learned of the other hijackings. Several Middle Eastern looking men had just stood up and it looked like they were taking over this plane as well. Convinced that they were part of the same group of Arab hijackers and that they would suffer the same fate, when they realized that their flight had been hijacked as well, a group of passengers stormed the terrorists taking over their plane and caused it to spin out of control and crash into the field. It was later established that this plane had been headed for the White House.

In little more than one and a half hours, these religious fanatics murdered thousands of innocent civilians. In all, more than three thousand people lost their lives. in this wonton act of madness. Those nineteen terrorists responsible for the attacks were Islamists, religious extremists of Arab descent. Fifteen of the hijackers were from Saudi Arabia, where members of the Saud royal family were heavy contributors to mullahs who preached against anyone who did not believe in Islam. Provided with tens of millions of dollars in contributions, some of which actually came from the government of Saudi Arabia, the majority of Muslims respected these radical religious leaders. They set up religious schools in which they taught tens of thousands of Muslim children to hate the United States, Europe, and Israel. Calling anyone who was not a follower of the prophet Mohammed and Islam an infidel, these mullahs taught that all infidels should be put to death. Over decades, these radical religious teachers poisoned the minds of tens of thousands of children, teaching them to hate.

When the Soviets pulled out of Afghanistan, a group of Muslim fundamentalists known as the Taliban took over the government. In the years that followed, religious executions became commonplace. Many of these executions were performed center field in packed stadiums before scheduled soccer games. Women were not permitted to go to school and were governed by strict interpretations of the Koran.

Within this environment, operating with the explicit help and open support of the Afghan Taliban government, the leader of the Al Quada terrorist organization, a man named Osama, himself a Saudi multimillionaire, funded an organization to recruit and train thousands of extreme Islamists. He funded his worldwide terror group by extorting money from some of his wealthy Saudi countrymen. Osama also supported the paramilitary intimidation of ordinary Afghan farmers into growing poppies, which he then sold to international drug cartels. He bribed powerful members of the Taliban, and in return they allowed him to operate training camps and to use Afghanistan as a base of operations for terrorist acts against a wide range of U.S. and European targets.

In the weeks after the September 11 attacks, President Kelley stepped up and pulled the country together. It seemed as though he was everywhere promoting unity and defiantly declaring that the United States would seek out and kill those responsible for the September 11 attacks. Osama and his partners in the Taliban paid little attention to Kelley's rhetoric. Previous presidents had threatened the use of military action in response to terrorist attacks, but little if anything was ever done about it. The Taliban and Osama seriously misjudged this president. The United States stood more united than it had in decades. Old Glory was flown from cars and buildings that had never flown flags before. He delivered ultimatums to the Afghan Taliban to "turn over Osama or suffer the full might of the U.S. military." The U.S. message to its allies and foes alike was loud and clear: "Stand clear! The United States is about to teach these extremists a lesson. The president's message was unmistakable the Taliban will fall. No one can attack the United States without facing major consequences. President Kelley's popularity soared.

For weeks before the U.S. attacked, President Kelley made demands upon the Talliban that they needed to "turn over Osama or suffer the consequences." President Kelley delivered that message in dozens of ways through dozens of intermediaries. He sent the secretary of state on European tour where day after day the message was repeated. He had the defense secretary meet with his counterpart from several other nations to make sure they would not inadvertently interfere with our military buildup.

The president's message to the rest of the world was blunt and to the point. Nations and individuals within those nations either stood with the United States, against the terrorists who attacked innocent civilians, or they stood against the United States. Any group or government that lent aid or safe harbor to America's terrorist enemies would also be considered an enemy. The full economic and military might of the United States would be brought to bear against any terrorist group or any nation that supported the terrorists.

The whole world knew the United States military was incredibly superior, but few knew just how superior the U.S. military had become, with its adoption of the laser-and computer-guided smart bombs and other new technology. President Kelley was about to test his idea of morphing an old-fashioned military into a lightning-fast, technology-enhanced modern military that could accurately deliver incredible force to within a foot or so of its intended target.

For weeks before the United States invaded Afghanistan, President Kelley made demands upon the Taliban that they needed to "turn over Osama or suffer the consequences." President Kelley delivered that message in dozens of ways through dozens of intermediaries. The world press was daily running stories about U.S. strategic military moves in preparation for an action against the Afghan Taliban government.

The response from the Taliban was absolute defiance. They would not turn over Osama, nor would they be cowed by U.S. military threats. They stood behind their support of Osama! They even went so far as to threaten President Kelley's life if he persisted in his threat to remove them from power. The "line in the sand" was as clear as day. In diplomatic circles, the Taliban openly sent messages that threatened, "Should President Kelley invade, they would work to assassinate him." President Kelley stood his ground, and in fact raised the ante by openly stating that shortly the Taliban would not be in power.

With so much going on, President Kelley was so wrapped up in his everyday schedule that he failed to sense the dangers of the powerful forces working against him. With the September 11 attack now some eight weeks behind him and with all diplomatic efforts at a dead end, the president had some decisions to make that could affect all Americans. He summoned General Ron Huey to his office.

"General Huey," he said, "I've called you here this afternoon to ask you face to face, are you ready to implement our Afghan plan? This is it, General. I've decided we need to do this without further delay."

"We're ready to do whatever you order us to do, Mr. President," the general replied. "Our Special Forces are ready and prepared to carry out the mission you've laid out for them. And Mr. President, *they will be successful.*"

President Kelley wished Huey Godspeed and dismissed him with the instructions; "I have set up a direct line to the White House. I want you to use that line frequently to update me on everything. I want you to stay in direct contact with me. If you call and for some reason I'm unavailable, my brother Bobby will speak with you."

In contrast to the Gulf War a dozen years before, this war began without direct television broadcast. The plan was to surprise the enemy as much as possible. The enemy knew the U.S. was coming, but they didn't know when. The whole world knew the U.S. would retaliate after Taliban leader Omar insultingly rebuked the U.S. demands for turning over Osama. They simply either didn't believe it would happen, believing the U.S. would never attack such a small country, or they didn't have a clue as to when it would happen. Just as in the Gulf war 10 years before against Iraq, Taliban leaders publicly boasted that they would destroy the American military just as they did the Russians. Russia's attack on Afghanistan in the late 1980's ended in a humiliating Russian defeat at the hands of the Talliban. However, that defeat came with the direct help of the U.S. in supplying hand held stinger missiles as well as other military gear.

During the next several days, it became obvious that something was going on in Afghanistan. The Brits, the French, and several American news organizations had journalists stationed inside Afghanistan, embedded within units of the Northern Forces Army and the Kurdish resistance. Taliban forces, responding to Kurdish and Northern Alliance Forces troop movements, began to mass their own army along fronts in the north, the west, and the south as they had done with great success so many times before. The consolidation of Taliban forces along defined fronts gave U.S. Special Forces the opportunity to employ their devastating force. Calling upon the carrier-based fighter jets, the U.S. Special Forces moved in close to the enemy.

The U.S. coordinated air strikes were absolutely devastating to the Taliban army. The Taliban were defeated before they actually knew what was going on. The carnage was so intense that any moving vehicle became a death trap. Tanks, trucks carrying troops, or any concentration of troops were easy targets. U.S. fighter jets took out the small Taliban air force without incident. Without air support, it didn't take long for the Taliban army to realize what was going on. The army scattered and ran for their lives, making them even more vulnerable to U.S. attack. The Kurdish forces and the Afghan Northern Alliance forces cleaned up the devastated Taliban Army in two and a half weeks.

As the outcome became obvious the implementation of the president's plan to revamp the military was now just a matter of time. In pole after pole of voters, President Kelley's popularity soared while his enemies secretly joined forces and conspired to kill him. They would do anything not to submit to his changes to their military.

One-star Brigadier General Ron Huey, the man in command of the entire Afghan operation, was a fifty-year-old graduate of West Point. Along with a dozen or so younger, more progressive-thinking generals, Huey was handpicked by President Kelley to coordinate the Afghanistan invasion. The plan called for the newly appointed generals to command twelve highly trained units, each consisting of twelve men equipped with the latest satellite technology. The old-line generals, who had fought previous wars, thought President Kelley was stark-raving mad. How could 144 or 288 well-trained warriors defeat a sovereign nation?

According to the president's plan, as proposed by General Huey, fighter and bomber pilots would circle for hours over the proposed area of conflict. The Special Forces units would directly contact this superior air power via satellite phones. The satellite phone transmissions would be beamed from the satellite to the aircraft carrier and relayed directly to the pilot. Software would ensure a seamless connection from fighter plane to aircraft carrier to satellite and back to ground forces. In effect, pilots commanding incredible destructive force would have eyes on the ground directing their programmed guided missiles.

By pointing a hand held specially designed gun that "shot" an infrared satellite-connected beam at the desired target, a method dubbed by the military as "painting," U.S. Special Forces could paint the location of the proposed target or targets, and that coordinate was beamed to the satellite. The satellite, using GPS technology, would then send that information directly to the computers on board the military jets, within a minute or so of their "painting." For the first time in the history of warfare, a ground commander could direct enormous destructive force with pinpoint accuracy. The plane's computers would lock onto the targets and launch smart bombs, computerized missiles programmed by the planes' computers to strike the "painted" target. This system had such amazing accuracy that it could deliver incredible destructive force within feet of a target.

When compared to air strikes in previous wars, where it took hundreds of bombs to carpet bomb a target to increase the chances of hitting a desired target, and then additional fly-over to determine the success of the air strike, the new system would produce direct hits with a single bomb in over 90 percent of the strikes. With an immediate assessment of the damage done to the target by those who painted the target, the guesswork was eliminated.

For a particularly fortified target, pilots could program one missile to strike the target, penetrating its outer shell, then launch another one or two missiles seconds behind the first. These missiles would hit the exact same spot and penetrate deeply into the target destroying even the most fortified targets.

Ground commanders could then communicate damage reports directly to the planes. If another pass or even several more strikes were needed, the pilots would know immediately.

There was never any doubt what the outcome of the U.S. invasion of Afghanistan would be, but most of the world was not prepared to witness this nation's awesome military power. Over a few short years, technology had changed so dramatically, that the world was stunned at the speed with which the United States defeated the Taliban. For a dozen years, those who opposed the Taliban had waged a civil war against them with little success. But with 144 Special Forces soldiers and the tremendous power they were able to direct against the enemy, the United States was able to bring the defiant Taliban down in a little more than two weeks.

Where the old-line generals wanted to mass tanks and manpower to defeat the Taliban, Huey counted on using the Kurdish Army, the Northern Alliance forces and other opposition forces to clean up the devastated Taliban Army without deploying very many American ground forces.

President Kelly's military victory was so complete and so overwhelming that the generals and intelligence officials who opposed Kelley became convinced they were on the losing side of the issue. The handwriting was on the wall; they had witnessed a new era in the history of waging war. Their sacred cow, Defense Department spending, was shifting out of their hands. They now realized that their careers would wind down as President Kelley appointed his handpicked officers to head up the changes that were about to take place in the military.

No longer in control of spending, not only would the old guard officials lose their power, they would also not be able to direct lucrative contracts to the defense contractors they were counting on securing highly paid positions with in their retirement. They had to do something, and they had to do it fast. The good of the national interest now took a back seat to their own personal financial interests. Their personal interests were now allied with the personal interests of the defense contractor CEOs, the intelligence community and the Mafia.

After the Taliban fell, many mid-and high-level Afghan government officials were interrogated by U.S. military intelligence. Keenly aware of the shift in power many of these officials were friendly to the new wave of generals that would now quickly rise in rank to take over leadership of the U.S. military. Intelligence officers learned from these Afghan officials of the secret bribes and information leaks instigated by Allen Dunlap. President Kelley was meeting with the Secretary of Defense Jim Hill along with several of Hill's aides when one of his aides interrupted the meeting.

"Mr. President you have an urgent call on your direct line." "Thank you Bill, I'll be right there. Excuse me for a few minutes Jim, we need to continue this discussion but I need to take this call" the President responded.

"Mr. President, I have just absolutely confirmed what we had suspected about those reports I gave you last week about the CIA," the general said. "Director Dunlap's in this up to his neck. His top people have been feeding military detail to the Taliban. I've just confirmed that a story I planted with loose tongues at the Pentagon, the story you and I spoke of about the 2nd Armored Division, well, Sir, it did in fact go to the Taliban. When I confronted the men responsible, and they realized what they were doing, some of Dunlap's own people gave him up."

"General that news doesn't surprise me but it does sadden me. I had hoped what we suspected wasn't true," the president responded. "Thank you general, you have done a great service to our country."

For weeks President Kelley and General Huey had suspected that sensitive military information was being leaked to the Taliban, so they planted a story to see if it found its way into the enemy's hands. In his support of the military status quo, and against the president's shakeup of the military, CIA Director Dunlap had given instructions to his field operatives that were in direct conflict with the president's policies. This could be considered treason. President Kelley summoned Director Dunlap to his office.

CHAPTER 8

▼

BURNING BRIDGES,
POWERFUL ENEMIES

"Mr. President, Director Dunlap is here to see you." "Thank you, Susan. Please show him in."

Kelley previously had asked one of his most trusted Secret Service agents, a man named Rufus Youngblood, to station himself immediately inside the Oval Office within earshot of the conversation he would have with Dunlap. When the Director walked into the president's office and began to close the door behind him, he expected agent Youngblood to step outside. Dunlap was unaccustomed to having Secret Service agents in the room when he was speaking with the president. Most of the briefings he gave the president were top secret. When Youngblood didn't move, Dunlap looked at the president as if waiting for him to ask Youngblood to step outside. It was an awkward moment that seemed far longer than it actually was when Dunlap asked the Secret Service agent to step outside.

"I've asked agent Youngblood to be present for this meeting," the president said. Dunlap sensed immediately that this was not going to be a typical meeting. The president began the conversation. "I asked you here today because I want an explanation. Why are you leaking information about our military campaign in Afghanistan?"

Dunlap responded, "Mr. President, why would I do something like that? I'm doing no such thing. Where did you get such information?" "Look, I've known for quite some time that you have been working with a group of over-the-hill generals and that you have been instructing Afghan field operatives in your agency to work against my stated policy."

Dunlap vehemently denied the president's accusations. But President Kelley had had enough. He mustered all the patience could, then in a civil demeanor said to Dunlap, "get up out of that chair and get your sorry ass out of my office. I have arranged to have you escorted back to your office by three FBI agents. You're fired! Clear your personal effects out of your office, and leave."

The president told Dunlap that all his access to privileged government files, including access to government buildings, would be denied immediately.

"I'm going to call a news conference," the president continued. "During this news conference, I will announce that you and several generals who will be resigning their commission immediately have been working to establish a military agenda contrary to that of my administration. You and your Pentagon conspirators have been working to undermine the United States military in its mission to defeat the Afghan Taliban."

In a move of total defiance, Dunlap turned as he exited the Oval Office and raised his voice at the president. "Who in the hell do you think you're talking to? You and your group of northeastern rich boys come in here and don't know your ass from a hole in the ground! You need to know directly from my lips, that I will not rest until I get even with you. I have worked my whole life in service to my country, and I won't allow you to destroy that. This is far from over!"

Rufus Youngblood was a huge man, six foot four inches, two hundred forty pounds; he firmly grasped Dunlap by the arm and turned his body toward the door. He escorted Dunlap back to his office and then followed him to make sure he left the premises. Reporting back to the president, he said, "Mr. Dunlap was quite upset, Sir. He was voicing obscenities about you and saying how he would get even if it was the last thing he did." Youngblood composed a report capturing the president's entire meeting with Dunlap, emphasizing the open physical threats made against the president. The report eventually made its way up the command and to the office of the FBI director.

Not only did the Kelleys burn a number of bridges in their rise to power, the president's father had stepped on quite a few toes on his way to fame and fortune. Among the president's enemies were some very powerful men: congressmen; CEOs of some of the largest companies in the world, including defense contractors; Mafia bosses; union presidents; and four-star generals.

During prohibition, the president's grandfather, after trying to corner the market on Scotch, had narrowly avoided being marked for death by the powerful

Luciano crime family. Using his political influence, which extended into the White House, Joe Kelley openly competed against Mafia whiskey imports from Scotland. Although he was warned repeatedly by low-ranking Mob people, Kelley made exclusive deals with Scottish distilleries. Upon taking delivery of the Scotch, he stored it in warehouses so the supply would dwindle and the price rise. Joe Kelley Sr., like his grandsons years later, simply didn't understand the powerful enemies he was cultivating. He was the kind of person who was accustomed to thumbing his nose at others. As a former ambassador with substantial political connections, he frequently flaunted his position at the expense of others. With his vast fortune and political connections, he could pressure people into giving him his way in most business deals.

The senior Kelley only relented to Charlie "Lucky" Luciano after finding out that he was about to be killed, but not before having cost Luciano hundreds of thousands of dollars. Charlie Luciano was not the kind of person to disrespectfully thumb your nose at. He was the head of a ten-billion-dollar organization. He would just as soon kill a competitor as compete with him; either way all he had to do was order what he wanted. They were well organized and as professionally managed as any fortune 100 company. With over 5,000 "soldiers," "made men" who were anxious to please their Capo, all it took was a nod or a word and people died. Luciano was livid and vowed revenge against Joe Kelley.

"Isn't this the same creep I've seen on the front pages of all the newspapers whoring around Hollywood with these big-time movie actresses?" Luciano asked his partner, Frank Costello. "He's married and has a bunch of kids too. I've read about this big-shot Wall Street guy. He creates these financial schemes and takes advantage of small investors, lining his own pockets. Have you ever met him, Frank?" Frank shook his head. "No, Charlie. But I did speak with him to give him your message that he would never live to see his plan to corner the market for Scotch distribution in this country come true."

"You know, Frank, I don't even know the guy and I don't like him. He's the kind of guy who'll buy his way into anything he wants. I don't want his money in restitution; I'll get even with him when it means the most to him. I'm going to teach this arrogant, disrespectful Irish bastard a lesson."

Now, years later, Kelley's grandsons had screwed the successors to these Mob leaders. Knowing that his son could win his bid for election to the presidency with the help of organized labor unions, Joe Kelley had asked for a meeting with Sam Gicondo, a powerful Chicago Mafia boss. Jack Kelley would need to carry Illinois, West Virginia, and Ohio, and Joe Kelley knew that Sam Gicondo could tilt the union vote in those states and several others in favor of his son. Thinking they could make a sweet deal for themselves with the Kelleys in the White House, several Mob families joined forces and agreed to help Joe Kelley and his son win the presidency.

Meeting on a golf course at an out-of-the-way private club in West Virginia, Joe Kelley, Sam Gicondo, internationally known singer Frankie Singaro, and an actor who was married to one of Joe Kelley's daughters sealed their deal. Jack could count on a heavy union vote. The Kelleys promised that once they won the presidency they would be non aggressive and even friendly behind the scenes when it came to enforcing the federal government's efforts against union corruption and other Mob-friendly businesses.

Mob bosses ordered unions in key states to get behind Jack Kelley for president. During the primaries, they made sure Kelley would win in state after state by stuffing the ballot box with union votes. A year or so after the election, it was learned that on election day they had seen to it that one hundred thousand deceased citizens had voted for Kelley in Cook County, Illinois, and Hudson County, New Jersey. In election districts all over the country, they turned a close election against a sitting vice president in favor of Kelley.

With the election behind him, his son having won the presidency, a prize Joe Kelley had dreamed about most of his adult life, Jack appointed his brother, Bobby, Attorney General. Again with total disregard for the deal they had made and with total disrespect for the people they made that deal with, Kelleys' sons, with a holier-than-thou attitude, went after the Mafia with a vengeance. In the first two years of the Kelley administration, the Justice Department under Attorney General Robert Kelley indicted over 350 Mafia figures.

At first skeptical that it was some sort of government scam, these enraged Mob bosses became eager players when approached by CIA/FBI operatives seeking their help in getting rid of President Kelley. As if to rub salt in the Mafia's wounds, the Kelley brothers, like their father and grandfather before them, were known as being womanizers. They were sexually passing around the girlfriend of Sam Gicondo, the Chicago Mob capo. Giacondo was furious and vowed revenge.

Another high-ranking Mob capo whose father was originally in the Luciano mafia family was Carlo Marcello from New Orleans. Marcello senior enjoyed a close, personal relationship with Frank Costello and Lucky Luciano. Costello got behind Marcello early on and set him up with an extension of his gambling business. Costello made sure all Mob interests in the New Orleans region knew that Marcello was operating with and through his family. Over the years Marcello and his friends became fabulously wealthy, extending Marcello's influence into prostitution, unions, and other organized crime activities. Now an old man, Marcello brought his son in to take over.

With little advance warning, Marcello was picked up by immigration authorities at the urging of Attorney General Kelley and deported. Months later, having won his legal battle and once again in the United States, Marcello, a calculating, deliberate, and ruthless Mob boss, also vowed revenge. He told his son he would "strike the head, not the tail" of his enemy—he would go after Jack, not Bobby. Some three years into the Kelley administration the heads of three major crime families were discussing how they might take down these arrogant brothers.

In early March 2003, under the guise of discussing national defense issues, a small group of generals secretly met with senior intelligence officers from the CIA, DIA, and FBI. The six men openly discussed how they might eliminate the president. Some of them justified their talk by reminding the others of specific presidential acts that they believed compromised national interests. The assistant director of the FBI chimed in, "I'm sure you all know that Kelley is so brazen in his womanizing escapades that he openly has frequent sexual rendezvous in the White House itself." Another gave an account of how the president and his brother were swapping back and forth between them the mistress of Sam Giacondo.

"I'll bet Giacondo isn't too happy about that," one of the generals said. "He may even be pissed off enough we might be able to use him. The Mafia might allow all of us to play a behind-the-scenes role in getting rid of Kelley. Then if something goes wrong, we can point to them. God knows with all the bad blood between the Kelleys and the Mob over the years, they certainly have plenty of reason to kill him. Bill, your people at CIA have had dealings with these Mafia guys in the past. Why don't you make some serious but discreet inquiries into this. If we can get these guys on board, they would provide us with all the cover we need if anything goes wrong."

Before the meeting broke up, the men discussed how each saw the ascension of Vice President Jones to the Presidency. The intelligence people at the meeting reported that the ongoing investigations into corruption within the VP's circle of aides were threatening to become public, and the vice president knew he could ill afford such a scandal. Knowing that the vice president feared being dropped from the ticket in the presidential race that was less than a year away, the men agreed to approach the vice president through his longtime friend and trusted aide, Billy Esters. The meeting broke up on the suggestion that they would get together again in two weeks after seeking Mafia involvement and making an initial approach to Billy Esters.

By the end of March, initial conversations with the Mafia and Billy Esters had taken place, and the same group convened for another meeting. This time they brought in Esters and two-high ranking Mafia captains. "What can we expect from the VP, Billy?" asked Air Force General Curtis Mays.

Esters reported, "The VP was quite cautious when I first presented this, but he saw it as his opportunity to be president and change the direction President Kelley has pointed this country in. He has come to believe that the only way he will go down in history as a great man is to get out from under the political dominance of these northeastern elitists he has grown to hate."

"That said, however, and in an abundance of caution, he wants you to know that he will not take a direct part in these efforts, but will work with you behind the scenes to make it happen and then frustrate any legitimate attempt to get to the bottom of the assassination, in effect covering it up."

That was music to everyone's ears. This was also an extremely important issue for the Mob capos. These were street-wise, high-ranking Mafia leaders who themselves had to kill to rise through the ranks. They would be able to report to their bosses, the dons of their families, that they had met with generals and senior intelligence people to discuss the assassination of Jack Kelley and that the man who would become the next president was on board with a promise to cover the whole thing up. Their motive was strictly revenge. It was time to get even for the Kelleys betrayal.

"Mr. Salvatore, what do you think?" asked one of the generals.

"Well, you realize that we must get final approval of anything we say we might be able to do. But I will say this, if you can set this up, we will do it free of charge. I would expect you to pay our out-of-pocket expenses. We figure we would need about a million dollars to handle the mechanics of the operation. This is not your typical hit. Whoever does this is going to want some assurances that we can cover him, and that's not going to be cheap. If you can give me your assurance that our expenses will be paid up front, and that what I heard here today is the way it will go down, I can assure you that our answer will be in your hands within twenty-four hours."

"Mr. Salvatore," said the CIA operative, "I can cover the million dollars out of my covert account, so the money is no problem. If your answer is affirmative, we will need a certain level of communication about how you intend to do this.

"We will tell you how and when once we know Kelley's schedule. You will then need to fit into our plans," Salvatore replied.

The following morning the CIA chief had his answer from Mr. Salvatore. Under the circumstances discussed at the meeting, they would do the job.

For his part, Vice President Jones would convince President Kelley to "mend political fences" by going to Texas. From the early days of their administration, the Kelley brothers, using the power of the Federal Government, jumped into the middle of several issues that caused much dissent in the Bible Belt South. In a confrontation that made national headlines for several weeks, Kelley backed away from having the federal government challenge several states that had passed legislation allowing gay marriage. Most southerners thought Kelley betrayed their religious beliefs by sending in his legislative aides to several states to help craft legislative language that resulted in laws allowing gays to marry. Many had voted for him because they thought he shared their moral and ethical beliefs. If Kelley were to be reelected, carrying the South would be a must. This part of the country was Jones's home turf, and though he would never be directly involved, he could arrange whatever needed to be done to help the assassins accomplish their goal. Texas was friendlier than any other state in meeting the need for secrecy. Everyone was now in place. Not only could they kill the President they could get away with it.

Giacondo reached out to his counterpart in a New York crime family, and they arranged for three experienced hit men from Corsica to do the job. The hit men would position themselves in Dealey Plaza so that they would have Kelley's limo in crossfire, high, low, and the middle. Giacondo and his counterpart split the million dollars evenly. They paid each shooter five kilograms of heroin; the hit men could sell the drug a little at a time anywhere in the world, and never have to work again. The Corsican Mafia was chosen because of its' ruthlessness in enforcing A Morta, the code of silence. The assassins knew their whole family would die if they broke the code.

Arrangements were made for the Corsicans to fly into Mexico City, where they would be picked up and driven to a rented safe house in Dallas. Complete with plenty of food and expensive wine, they would cook their favorite dishes and drink their wine for a total of three weeks. No restaurants, no bars—except for daily visits to the plaza, they were to stay in the safe house. They were driven by two Mafia soldiers, "made men" who themselves killed at the command of their ranking family heads. The two were given strict instructions governing their behavior; they knew they would die if they screwed up this contract. They made the long trip to Mexico City and then to Dallas in their own car leaving no rental car paperwork or airline ticket to trace them to the killers. The Corsicans' trip from Rome would not be traceable beyond Mexico City.

The hired killers arrived on November 12. On ten consecutive days they went to Daily Plaza to walk off how many feet it was from one position to another.

One at a time they agreed on the three positions they would take, each casing the area for the best escape route. After the murder, they would go back to the safe house and stay there for two weeks, until the furor subsided. So they wouldn't have to deal with the tightened security typical of U.S. airports since the 9/11 attacks, they would then be driven to Toronto where they would catch a plane back to Italy and Corsica. Usually after high level hits such as this, the shooters were themselves whacked so there was no way to trace where they came from. In this case, they demanded and received assurances from the highest levels of the Mob families involved that no such thing would happen. The CIA and other coconspirators had arranged for a patsy to take the blame. The Corsicans could do their job without worrying about what would happen once they completed their deadly plans.

CHAPTER 9

▼

THE AWAKENING

Just as Bobby was about to head home for the evening, his phone rang. It was Sean McDonald, his voice quivering with excitement.

"I need you to call me on my other line immediately. I have good news, Bobby!"

"Give me ten minutes to get to an outside phone," Bobby said. He left his office and drove down the street to a pay phone to call Sean on his private number.

"What is it, Sean?" Bobby asked.

"Great news, Bobby! I've just received a call from one of my men who was on duty guarding Jack." Sean was unable to contain himself. "He's awake, Bobby! He's awake"!

"Calm down, Sean. Tell me all the details. Is he OK? Has he spoken to anyone? Is he coherent?"

"He seems to be fine, according to the duty officer. He's asking questions about what happened. He doesn't have any recollection of that day after getting into the limo. His voice is weak and he struggles, but he's asking about his family and seems to be alert."

Bobby hung up the phone after telling Sean he would make arrangements to fly to Dallas immediately. Then he called the man who had served as the family pilot for years and instructed him to get a plane ready for a trip to Reno, Nevada. He told the pilot not to file a flight plan; he would be there in about two hours.

Arriving home to pack an overnight bag, he quietly motioned his wife, Nancy, to follow him into the backyard. "What is it Bobby" Nancy wanted to know?

"Jack is out of his coma, and he seems to be fine. He's asking questions about what happened," Bobby whispered.

"Oh, thank God!" Nancy said. "It's been so long I was beginning to wonder if he would ever come out of it. What's going to happen now?"

"Honey, I'm not 100 percent sure. I know it's hard for you having me away so much of the time, but these next few weeks will even be worse. Bear with me, and please don't worry. It will all work out fine. I'm on my way to Texas."

"How long will you be gone?"

"Just a day or two. I should be home either Saturday or Sunday night. I have several meetings on Monday morning at the office, so I'm hoping no later than Sunday afternoon." Bobby beamed. "This is incredible, isn't it?"

"Just remember you're dealing with murderers, Bobby, and please be careful. What would I ever do if something happened to you? Call me as soon as you think you can"

Next Bobby called his sister-in-law in Georgetown to let her know he was on his way over. Jackie instinctively knew that something was going on. Full of anticipation, she opened the door to greet her brother-in-law. Bobby kissed her on the cheek as he hugged her.

"Jackie, I'm so excited! I had to come here before I went out of town. Jack is awake and asking for you and the kids."

Jackie broke down, tears spilling from her eyes as Bobby explained to her that Jack was weak but lucid and aware.

"When will I be able to see him?" Jackie wanted to know. "These past months have been pure hell, thinking about my husband lying in a coma thousands of miles away, not knowing if he was going to live or die. Do you have any idea what this has been like for me and the kids, Bobby? Every time they ask me when daddy's coming home, I want to just sit down and cry."

Bobby reached out and took Jackie's hand in his "Jackie, I know how difficult these months have been for you, but I think this is the beginning of the end of the hell these people have put us through. I love Jack too, and this has not been easy for any of us. I'm on my way to Dallas now. I'll keep you informed, and I promise you can visit him very soon. You know how dangerous this is. The next few weeks will be critical. Just give me a chance to see what's going on and figure out how I can arrange your visit." With that Bobby embraced her again, kissed her on the cheek, and promised, "I'll call you in the next day or so."

A short time later, Bobby was on a Learjet climbing quickly to 20,000 feet in the clear summer night. Within minutes of takeoff Bobby walked up to the cockpit and said to the pilot, "Mickey, we have to switch plans. We're going to Dallas now. Can you make the necessary adjustments?"

Bobby knew that it would only be a few days, a week at most, before he'd have to move his brother to a more private place. But he also knew that it was only a matter of time now before they would go public with all they knew about the treacherous events of last November 22. He had had eight months to plan how they would execute his brother's re-emergence, eight months during which to accumulate evidence regarding the cover up, now that Jack was out of his coma it was finally time to do it and he relished the idea of getting even with all who were involved in this.

Moving Jack to another location was a very dangerous proposition. It would mean an ever-increasing group of people would know he was alive. Sean, Bobby, and the others were terrified about the possibility of a leak getting back to those responsible for the assassination attempt. They would have to be extremely careful about who they allowed to help them move on to the next step in Jack's recuperation. Until now only a small handful of trusted and dedicated men had been entrusted with the secret that the President had survived the assassination attempt.

As Bobby settled into his seat for the flight to Dallas, the seriousness of taking these next steps to protect Jack began to sink in. He began thinking about the problems facing them now that Jack was out of the coma. Those responsible for the attempted assassination would stop at nothing if they knew the president was alive.

Bobby's mind skipped from one thing to another as the plane sped along on its route to Dallas. He was almost jumping out of his skin with excitement at the prospect of seeing his brother and having him back again. The only thing that was important to Bobby now was that Jack was going to be OK. But even in all the excitement, he knew he needed to be levelheaded and very careful about how he handled every detail about Jack's reemergence into the public eye. Eight months before, during Jack's elaborate funeral, an event attended by heads of state from dozens of nations, famous people gave eulogy after eulogy, all but canonizing Jack. Bobby knew the public, even those who voted for Richard Dixon, would be outraged at those who had tried to murder their beloved president. At the same time Bobby was hopeful the public would understand why he had remained silent all these months, and why he put the country through the emotionally wrenching experience of bidding farewell to their leader.

Bobby decided that when the proper time presented itself, he would ask his wealthy friend Robert Wood to allow them to use Wood's Georgia estate for the final leg of his brother's recuperation. The president and Bobby had been invited to the estate to go quail hunting with Mr. Wood several times. It was a four-hundred-acre farm about twenty-five or thirty miles outside Atlanta, not far from Emory and Northside Hospitals, two sophisticated medical centers where talented physicians were on staff should Jack need them.

The Wood estate was an easily secured place should their enemies make another attempt on the President's life. The main house was a completely renovated 140-year-old mansion that somehow survived the burning of Atlanta in 1865, when General Sherman had destroyed everything in a forty-mile wide path as his army made its way to Savannah. No detail had been overlooked in the modernization of the 25,000-square-foot mansion. It had a state-of-the-art security system that not only protected the main house and the immediate area around the main house, but that also extended through the twenty-five or so acres that had been cleared around the house.

With sensors, security cameras, and motion detectors everywhere, the estate was perfect for providing Jack a secure and comfortable place to further regain his strength. He was all but positive Wood would not refuse his request. Sean and his men would need to recruit several more men from their squad to secure the estate against intrusion. Sean and several of his men would have to arrange time off, taking vacation time so they could act as a constant core security group, with other members coming in and out of the schedule.

The plan for announcing to the public that Jack was still alive would need to be formulated and finalized with several members of the Antonio group's inner circle. Every detail would need to be carefully considered, and paramount in the planning was the all-important need for secrecy, at least for the next few weeks. After landing in Dallas and before getting into his waiting limousine, Bobby instructed the pilot to refuel the plane. Then, wanting to avoid using the hospital's main entrance and following Sean's advice, he asked the limo driver to park near a secondary hospital entrance and wait there to take him back to the airport. As he climbed out of the limo he told the driver it would be anywhere from an hour to two hours before he returned.

As Bobby got out of the car and walked toward the hospital entrance, he saw a familiar-looking man walking toward him. "Oh God," he thought, "is that Congressman Smith?" G. Michael Smith was the ranking member of the House Intelligence Committee. He was a consummate politician, and he made it his business to know something about everyone's business. Being the ranking member on intelligence, he took his job very seriously, serving his country well by being on the "inside" of so many issues.

"What a bad sign," Bobby thought. "Of all the people to run into, Smith was at the top of the list of those to avoid." Yet here he was walking right toward him. Smith was a Texas congressman with close political ties to President Jones. He was with the vice president on the day of the assassination, and had left the hospital and traveled back to Air Force One with Jones that day. Bobby knew that Smith would almost certainly mention seeing Bobby in Dallas the next time he talked to the president, and he knew that with President Jones that would arouse suspicion. The last thing Bobby wanted was someone snooping around trying to figure out why he was in Dallas.

"What in the world are you doing here Bobby?" Smith asked as the two men met.

Trying to conceal his nervousness, Bobby explained, "I had a meeting here in town and had been informed that a close friend of the family, actually a second or third cousin, was a patient at the hospital, so I thought I'd stop in to say hello. And what brings you here, Michael?"

"My brother had his gallbladder removed yesterday. I was paying him a visit," Michael said. He tried to engage Bobby in conversation about the upcoming release of the Werner Commission assassination report. "Will I see you Thursday when the Werner Report is released?" he asked.

Bobby politely deflected the answer, saying, "I'm not really privy to most of the commission's findings. From what I hear about how the commission has conducted its business, there will be key parts of the report I simply won't agree with. I don't want to appear to lend credence to the report's findings by being present at its release, I'm sure you understand."

"Well Michael, I've got to run, I'll see you back in Washington. This is the last weekend for the next several that I'll be able to relax, I'm on a really tight schedule, I've got to be back in DC for a Monday morning meeting." Smith then asked, "Will you be attending the signing ceremony when the president signs into law your brother's tort legislation"? Jack had introduced this bill the year before, and President Jones, using his skill as the former majority leader in the Senate, had brilliantly guided it through Congress.

Bobby again politely sidetracked, a direct answer by asking, "When is the signing ceremony?"

"This coming Tuesday," Smith said. "I think I'm in San Francisco Tuesday, but I'll check. Maybe I'll see you there."

"If memory serves, I think I'll see you next Friday," Bobby said. "Don't we meet with President Jones to discuss the terrorist bill he is planning to introduce?"

"I think you're right. I'll see you then."

As the two men bid farewell and started to walk away, Smith turned back and with a slightly elevated tone in his voice he called, "Give my regards to Jackie!"

"I will Michael," Bobby called back, "take care, I'll see you soon"! In the hospital, as he got on the elevator and pushed the button for the fifth floor, Bobby took out a pen and jotted down a note reminding himself to see if Smith's brother was in fact in the hospital. The chance encounter with Smith changed everything.

"I can't leave Jack here for another day," he thought. "I'd better arrange for a trip to Atlanta and have a conversation with Robert Wood."

Bobby took out his cell phone and placed a call to his friend. "Robert how are you?" Bobby asked "Is that you Bobby? What a pleasant surprise to hear from you, I'm fine. To what do I owe this call so late on a Friday evening? Is everything alright?" Bobby explained "I need your friendship more now than I ever have before," he said to Wood. "I can't go into great detail right now, but I need you to trust me when I say that this is extremely important to me and my entire family. Would you be kind enough to allow a very special guest to stay at the mansion for several days? I promise you'll understand why when you know the whole story."

"You're like a son to me, Bobby. I have always had a very warm feeling for you, and you know I loved your brother as if he were my son. Of course you can make my home your home," Wood replied. "When will you be needing my hospitality"?

The answer came quickly. "This evening, Robert." "Where are you now, Bobby?"

"I'm about two hours from you, Robert. I should get there between 10:30 and midnight depending on what kind of time we make."

"I'll have my housekeeper prepare your rooms. I'm looking forward to seeing you. Will you be driving or flying?"

"We'll be landing at DeKalb-Peachtree Airport," Bobby answered.

"I'll have my limo waiting for you in the parking lot in front of the Downwind Restaurant. Just ask anyone where it is," Wood said.

"That's great, Robert. I can't tell you how much this means to me. And Robert, I know it'll only be a few hours until I get there, but I would appreciate it if you didn't mention to anyone that I called. You'll understand why when I get there."

Hartsfield Airport is on the south side of Atlanta, it's one of the busiest airports in the world, it would not have been the first choice for landing as it is a major hub for connecting flights and Bobby didn't want to chance bumping into someone. Besides the Peachtree Dekalb Airport (PDA) was 25 miles closer to the Wood estate than Hartsfield.

Not wanting to attract any more attention than he needed to, and following Sean's exact instructions, Bobby turned to the right after getting off the hospital elevator and acted as though he knew exactly where he was going.

It was after normal visiting hours, and several nurses looked at him as he walked by them on his way to room 515. Bobby wasn't sure if they recognized who he was or if they were simply looking at him because they knew he was a visitor and should not have been there at that time of night. Walking past a nurses' station, he made eye contact with one of the doctors standing there. Sean had arranged to have one of the doctors who were on board from the first day to be present at Bobby's arrival.

The doctor immediately walked up to Bobby. "I'm Dr. Clark," he said, as the men shook hands, "we've talked several times. I'm pleased to have finally met you. Follow me. I'm sure your brother will be excited to see you."

"Doctor I can't begin to thank you and your colleagues enough for all you've done for my brother and our family, we will be indebted to each of you for the rest of our lives. When the time is right and the opportunity presents itself we will more openly show just how much we appreciate what you have done".

Following the doctor into a hospital room, Bobby was relieved to see familiar faces. Not being able to visit the hospital for fear of attracting unwanted, attention Bobby had had to rely upon the conversations he had with Jack's doctors and security people. So upon entering the room he instantly felt peace of mind seeing these dedicated people. After eye contact with several of the Special Forces bodyguards, with nods of acknowledgement between them, Bobby went directly to his brother's bedside. Jack was sedated but awake enough to recognize his brother. Tears immediately came to both men's eyes. The past eight months had been eight months of hell for both brothers, Jack fighting for his very life and Bobby not knowing from moment to moment whether something he said or did would get both he and his brother killed. They didn't have to say what they were feeling; it showed on their faces.

Even while in a coma over these months, Jack's wounds were healing and in fact his doctors concerns mounted over the last few months not for his physical recovery but regarding his continuing coma. With each change of his head bandage, now some eight months after the assassination attempt, the doctors and nurses noted that Jack's hair had substantially grown back. The scar along the right side of his head was slowly starting to disappear beneath his chestnut red and brown hair. The scar in the lower part of his neck would take further corrective plastic surgery but the nasty looking scar although still a pinkish standout against his fair complexion was now healed.

Bobby leaned over Jack and delicately put his arms around his brother, almost afraid to put any pressure on his brother's delicate body. Bobby spent several minutes bent over his brother, whispering in his ear as the tears ran down their faces.

"How is Jackie?" was the president's first question.

"She misses you terribly," Bobby whispered. "I stopped by her town home to let her know you had finally woken up, before I caught the plane to come here."

"Town home? What town home, Bobby?" Bobby continued to fill his brother in on the events of the past eight months.

"Well, she and the kids had to move out of the White House a few weeks after you were shot. Jones naturally wanted to move his family in. But the son of a bitch, for all his treachery, really didn't treat Jackie badly at all. Jackie and the kids moved back into your Georgetown town home, it was familiar, comfortable and immediately available. You do remember the town home you purchased when you were in the senate, don't you?" Bobby asked. "Yes, of course I do, I guess I just didn't think the whole thing through," Jack said "But wait until you hear what we've learned about the people who tried to kill you. Those things can wait, though. I'll fill you in about those things over the next several days", Bobby promised.

"What do my kids think happened to me? Are Carolyn and John OK?" the president pressed on.

"Jack, the kids are fine. Of course they don't understand why their daddy isn't there, and they miss you terribly. They ask about you every day. Carolyn graduated from kindergarten last month. Nancy and I went. We took pictures."

"When can I see Jackie and the kids?"

"We can't get too cocky here, Jack. We have to be extremely careful until you regain your strength. It's going to be a few more weeks before we can safely arrange a visit."

"Was Jackie hurt with any of the shots? "No Jack she's fine," Bobby responded. "How is the Governor? Who else was hurt? Who did this to me? Have they caught the gunmen"? The President had so much to catch up on, still hugging each other, their arms wrapped firmly around each other's shoulders, neither man wanted to let go.

Jack had many more questions, about Jackie and the governor and the men who'd shot him, but Bobby ignored them. "Jack, I've had months to think through how we should go public with all that has happened, and I'll discuss that and everything else you want to know over the next few days. In the meantime, I just bumped into Congressman Smith as I was coming into the hospital, so I can't leave you here. It's too dangerous. I know how weak you must be, but I've arranged for us to fly to Robert Wood's home in Atlanta. Do you feel up to it?"

"Whatever you say, Bobby. Just tell me what you want me to do. I'm just so happy to see you; I'm at a loss for words." Tears continued to roll down Jack's cheeks. "It's been a long time since I've said this, but I love you, Bobby. Thanks for being there for me."

"I love you too, Jack."

After answering the many personal questions Jack presented and that he now knew a rough outline about what was going on regarding attempts to kill him, Bobby wanted to reassure Jack and emphasized that both he and his family were well. The next several hours would be very tense. Getting Jack from Dallas to Atlanta and settled into Wood's estate would be physically exhausting for Jack and emotionally draining for Bobby. Bobby explained to his brother precisely how he planned to move him from the hospital.

Bobby was relieved to see that Jack remembered who Wood was and that he was responding well to the plan to move him to Georgia. After all, the doctors still had some concern about how his head injuries might have affected his thinking and memory.

"I'll be with you every step of the way, Jack," Bobby explained. "You remember Sean McDonald, don't you? Well, I've arranged to have a dozen of his Special Forces soldiers back us up with whatever force is necessary. But you're going to have to muster all the strength you have to make this trip. Simply walking from the car to the plane and from the plane to the car will take all your strength, even though you'll be in a wheelchair most of the time."

"After what I've been through, Bobby, you think I'd quit now? I can do it," Jack replied.

This would not be the first time Jack had to push his body to deliver more strength than it had to give. Jack had been a naval officer years before he was elected president. He had served his country valiantly in a number of hostile skirmishes, and had commanded a small naval vessel in the Pacific. During one battle the boat took enemy fire and was sunk. With the enemy searching the water for survivors, Jack and his crew of eight swam several miles to a deserted island. Jack was wounded, but he had to call upon every once of strength his body could muster or he would lose his whole crew.

Calling Dr. Clark off to the side, Bobby explained, "On the way into the hospital I bumped into a congressman who was leaving. Doc, I don't know if this guy is involved in the conspiracy or not, but I'm going to move the president to more secure surroundings."

"I don't know if the president is strong enough to be moved, Mr. Kelley," the doctor responded. "To make such a long trip less than a day after coming out of an eight-month coma, I don't know Bobby."

"But I don't have much choice, doctor. If I err, I'd rather err on the side of having Jack physically struggle than to be wrong and have these bastards try to finish their botched assassination."

This conversation took place as they were standing just a few feet away from Jack's bed, he overheard the conversation. "Let's do it, Bobby," said Jack in a soft, unassuming voice.

Bobby turned to look at his brother, smiled, and then turned back to the doctor. "There's our answer, doc." He then motioned to one of Sean's officers to help him swing Jack's legs around to the side of the bed and lift him into a waiting wheelchair.

Bobby wrapped several blankets around his brother and asked Dr. Clark if he would lead the way. No one would think twice about a patient being escorted by this prominent doctor who had been in residence at the hospital for nearly fifteen years. Moments before this, Dr. Clark had stepped out of the room and returned with a nurse. She would push the wheelchair, with the doctor escorting Jack, Bobby, and her, while three of the six Special Forces soldiers walked a short distance behind them. One of the remaining three soldiers was on the elevator as they wheeled the president on to it, and another was on the first floor waiting for the elevator to arrive, making sure no one interfered with the president's departure. Yet another was waiting at the limo for the entire group to arrive. Ever vigilant, they were trained to be ready for anything that might get in the way of their mission. They were to leave together for the trip to the plane and then on to Georgia.

The flight from Dallas was smooth and uneventful. They would arrive in Atlanta about 10PM and the trip to the Wood mansion would only take a half-hour or so. Everything seemed to be working according to the plan. Regardless of the risk, Bobby reasoned that leaving Jack in that hospital even for one more day after bumping into Congressman Smith would be far too risky.

Six members of the twelve-man team would travel with the president, and six were scheduled to join them in Georgia. Two of the Georgia six would meet the group at the DeKalb-Peachtree Airport. Much smaller than Hartsfield International but much larger than most suburban airports, DeKalb-Peachtree was a busy commercial airfield capable of taking all but the largest jets. Four members of the security group would travel to the Wood estate an hour or so before the president arrived. Their mission was to make sure the estate was secure and to set up secure perimeters. These four men were heavily armed, in full battle gear, ready to deal with anything that would potentially interfere with the well being of their commander-in-chief.

Waiting for his guests to arrive, and a little on edge with the suspense of not knowing who his soon-to-arrive guest was, Mr. Wood took a short walk around the gardens that surrounded his home. He was enjoying the warm summer evening, sipping from a glass of cognac as he strolled with one of his assistants. He made small talk about current political events, wondering what was so secretive about Bobby Kelley's request for the use of his mansion.

Wood was startled to see some men exiting a vehicle in the parking area a few hundred yards from where he stood. Four heavily armed men climbed out of the car and headed toward him. Wood's assistant was also a personal bodyguard, licensed to carry a gun. He slipped the 9 mm automatic pistol out of its holster and stepped several feet ahead of his boss.

As the four men approached, one of them said in an articulate, soft-spoken voice, "Mr. Wood, my name is Captain Lewis Cramer, United States Marine Corps. I apologize for the intrusion. I have been asked by Attorney General Robert Kelley to secure the premises for the arrival of your guest, sir. Would you please instruct your bodyguard to holster his weapon?"

Wood nodded at his assistant to put the gun away. More anxious than ever, he jokingly asked, "Who in the world is Mr. Kelley coming with, captain? The President of the United States?"

Captain Cramer simply smiled and said, "Mr. Wood, I know you're going to be very pleasantly surprised. We all thank you for being such a great American."

"Well, Captain, I guess I'll have to wait until the Attorney General arrives to find out who this mystery guest is. Go ahead and make whatever preparations you need to."

"Sir, one of the things we will have to insist upon," Captain Cramer continued, "is that any security people you have on the premises give up their weapons while your guest is here."

Turning to the bodyguard who was holstering his pistol, Captain Cramer said, "And that might as well start with you, sir." A little ticked off at the Captain's cocky attitude Mr. Wood's aid balked "I've been hired to provide protection for Mr. Wood and you have another thing coming Captain if you think I'm turning over my pistol." Captain Cramer turned to Mr. Wood and before he could say anything, sensing the potential seriousness of a confrontation, Wood told his bodyguard, "it's ok Bill, we know who these people are and it appears they are capable of dealing with any breach of security we might encounter, please allow these men to do their job and for the time being let them have your pistol."

Hoping to defuse the tenseness of the situation as he took the pistol from the bodyguard. Captain Cramer said "thank you sir, I have no intention of interfering with your obligation to protect Mr. Wood, but I do believe that when you are made fully aware of the seriousness of my mission, you will understand my concern."

"And you are not authorized to tell me who this guest of mine is?" Wood asked. "No sir, I'm not."

The military men had inside knowledge of what was happening in their country. They knew, having listened to the unfolding news events of the past eight months and being privy to the inside information their commanding officer shared with them, that powerful military officers in conjunction with civilians, including foreign civilians and powerful Mob figures, had attempted to take down their legitimate Commander in Chief. They were determined to lay down their lives if necessary to prevent that from happening. The future of their country was at stake, and they took it very seriously.

Robert Wood was the best kind of friend. While he didn't always agree with their politics, he had been friends with the Kelleys for decades before they won national office, and he trusted them. Even to the point of opening up his home to them.

For Jack, it was a long, tension-filled trip from Dallas. Jack had been through a terrible ordeal, and was groggy and physically exhausted. No doubt there was more to come, but for the moment he sat back and marveled at the number of stars in the heavens as they winged their way toward Atlanta at 24,000 feet on a cloudless July evening.

"Bobby, it's good to be out of the hospital," he said, leaning over to his brother, who was seated next to him. He motioned at the window. "You know, Bobby, it's amazing how much we take for granted. I know how sentimental I sound, but I can't wait to throw my arms around Jackie and have John and Carolyn jump on me while I'm lying on the floor. It's crazy the things you miss. And what would I ever do without my brother Bobby?"

"Now you're really getting down and dirty, Jack. Are you trying to make me cry?"

"No, I just want you to know how much I love you and appreciate you."

"Jack, I know how much you love me. And I also know that you would have done exactly the same for me if I'd been in the same circumstance. I'll bet we haven't told each other *I love you* more than two or three times in our entire life, and here we've said it twice in the past few hours. You know if this gets out you'll ruin my reputation for being ruthless." The brothers laughed for the first time in nearly a year.

"Let's get serious, Jack," Bobby said. "I've got so much to tell you about the bastards we're up against that I don't know where to begin." High above the lights from the cities below, the sky was aglow with tiny speckles of light from millions of stars. But the weakened president, exhausted by all that was going on, was unable to concentrate with the hum of the engines and rushing air, and his eyes began to close as he drifted off to sleep in the middle of a sentence.

It was a thirty-five-minute drive from the airport to the Wood estate, mostly on well-traveled highways. The estate would offer the president much more comfort than the hospital wing he left in Dallas. He would be able to freely walk the grounds, and not be confined to a bed or a room. This phase of the president's recovery required total relaxation, mild exercise, nutritious meals, and, above all, time. He would get all that on a first-class basis at the Wood estate. He was also nervously anticipating having Jackie visit him and spending some quiet time together. For now the kids would have to wait to be reunited with their dad, until the situation was no longer dangerous for them to be around their father.

At about 10:45 PM on a warm, cloudless summer evening, Jack and his entourage arrived at the estate of Robert Wood; the four security men who had arrived earlier standing with weapons ready some fifty to seventy-five feet away. Of course Wood full of anticipation as to whom Robert Kelley was bringing as his guest, was there to welcome his mystery guest. As the limo drove up the driveway and came to a stop in front of the main entrance to the mansion, the doors opened and several armed men exited, the last one pulling out a wheelchair. Bobby got out on the opposite side and walked around the car to help his brother out of the car and into the wheelchair. As Wood got a good look at the president's face, he gasped, not believing his own eyes. Tears immediately welled up in his eyes at the sight of the president. The man was considerably thinner then he remembered, and looked ashen white and a bit gaunt, but astonishingly this was Jack Kelley.

Eight months before he had attended the sad and solemn funeral of his beloved friend. He had been with the president from the very beginning, contributing hundreds of thousands of dollars to his election campaign. Now he wasn't sure what to say.

"Mr. President!" Wood exclaimed, overjoyed. He was so happy to see him he wanted to put his arms around his friend, but he could see how frail Jack was.

"Robert, thank you for allowing me to stay in your home. I hope this isn't a terrible inconvenience for you. As you can imagine, there weren't too many people we could trust with the knowledge that I was still alive." After a few incredibly warm and friendly pleasantries, Wood escorted Bobby and the exhausted president to the well-appointed guestrooms. Jack slipped into bed and with no effort at all, he drifted into slumber, his physical strength totally spent.

Wood was the only son of a man who had owned a vast empire founded upon carbonated beverages. He was in his mid-seventies and had long been accustomed to the finer things in life. He had taken his father's already incredibly successful business and with great skill and business acumen turned it into an internationally recognized empire worth billions of dollars. He was a lifelong Republican who contributed heavily to political causes he sympathized with. He had entertained Jack and Bobby at his home a number of times, inviting them to hunt quail with him, and he was a reliable and enthusiastic supporter of the president. The president and Wood, while separated some thirty years in age, had many common interests and genuinely enjoyed being with each other. Knowing Bobby Kelley as well as he did, Wood could tell by the way Bobby had asked for the use of his home that it was very important. Now having learned the identity of his guest, without hesitation Wood offered his support and fortune in helping Bobby in whatever way he could.

Right from the very beginning Robert Wood had suspected there was more than met the eye in the assassination of President Kelley, but he didn't know very much about the circumstances surrounding the many conspiracy theories that floated around in the hours and weeks after the assassination. Like many Americans, he watched the nonstop TV coverage on the capture of Osborn, but he couldn't believe that the authorities would let Osborn's killer get that close to a person in custody for the killing of a president. But he'd watched in horror as a man simply walked out of the crowd and shoved a gun into Osborn's stomach. He knew something was really wrong about the whole thing, but he wasn't a political person and never really believed there was a conspiracy. How could someone ever get away with killing a president without being exposed? Osborn must have done it, he reasoned. Now that he knew the president was alive and being protected, he wanted to find out the whole truth. He was actually angry that these guys actually got away with taking over the country.

After making sure that his brother was comfortably asleep, Bobby came back down to the den and joined Wood, who was sitting comfortably as if hoping that Bobby Kelley would join him. Wood was still sipping his cognac.

"Can I get you something to drink, Bobby?" he asked.

"Sure," Bobby replied, "I'll have what you're having."

During the conversation that ensued, Wood posed one question after another. Robert Wood was a billionaire and a very powerful man. He wanted to know all about the conspirators, and once again he pledged his total support in whatever the president needed.

"So what happens now, Bobby?" Wood asked.

"Well, we need to build Jack's stamina so we can go public with this and expose these sons of bitches," Bobby replied. "As soon as we can, I will arrange to have Jack do a nationally televised address to the nation, during which we will let the world know many of the details surrounding the assassination. How we do that will be the president's call," Bobby continued.

"You know, Bobby, I never did like that Jones guy. Somehow he always came off as a guy I would not trust in a business deal. But I'd bet good money that he isn't stupid enough to be involved in the assassination." Wood added, "Bobby, Jack can stay here as long as he likes. Remember if you need something Bobby, Atlanta is my town, I'd be honored to help you in anything you may need, just ask, ok"!

Still worried about Jack's mental state, Bobby wanted to be there when Jack awoke Saturday morning. After all he had been through, he was thrilled to have Jack back and apparently doing well. But for what Bobby had planned, Jack would not only have to build his physical strength, he would have to be up to his mental best. He only had Saturday and part of Sunday to bring Jack up to speed on all that went on during his months he was in the coma. It would be a lot to digest, but he wanted his brother to know everything.

It was nearly 11 AM Saturday morning when Bobby walked into Jack's bedroom to wake him. He had a pot of coffee and two cups in his hand.

"Wake up, Jack, you've been sleeping all day. Who the hell do you think you are, the president of the United States or something? Come on, get up, we have a lot of work to do," Bobby chided his brother.

Bobby had slept only four hours. He'd been up since 7 AM waiting for his brother to wake. He and Mr. Wood had sat for many hours the night before sipping cognac, discussing what was going to happen. Wood was a clearheaded, strategically thinking businessman, and he offered Bobby several insights into how they should handle a number of things. As it turned out, Wood's advice was invaluable.

Jack was visibly the worse off from the ordeal of coming out of an eight-month coma just that Friday afternoon and then having to travel that evening, even though his wounds were totally healed he was exhausted. So Bobby made sure Jack was focused before he began to lay out the early stages of his plan. "Jack, listen to me, you have to be up for this, it's very important," Bobby instructed his older brother. "Everything is under control. The main thing you need to do is rest, and in between resting get some mild exercise to build your muscles back into shape. But I need you to help me. You need to understand what we are up against."

"Of course, Bobby," Jack said.

"There are some things that you need to remember that even I don't know. You have been in meetings with some of these people when I wasn't there, so you're bound to have a different slant on some of these individuals. Let's start by going back to your meeting with the Joint Chiefs back in January of last year. Do you remember that meeting, Jack?"

"Yeah, I do. That was the meeting where I first unveiled my plan to cut back on their staffs. Boy, they didn't like that."

The brothers spent half of Saturday talking in Jack's room where he could discuss events surrounding November 22, while Jack rested in bed. Later that afternoon the president grew weary, so Bobby joined Robert Wood for an early dinner while Jack napped.

"How's it going Bobby? Is he responding well?" Wood asked as the two men sat down to a quickly prepared dinner of grilled rib eye.

"He is amazing," Bobby replied. "The doctors cautioned that I shouldn't expect him to be 100 percent mentally for at least several weeks. To be honest, I don't see any diminished mental capacity at all. He's grasping everything and remembering things from years ago."

"Isn't that great," Wood responded. After Jack awoke and had a bite to eat, the brothers went at it again, talking for several more hours late into Saturday evening.

Sunday morning they ate breakfast in Jack's room, where once again they huddled for hours with Jack resting in bed as they discussed every detail of the events leading up to the assassination and its subsequent cover-up. It was Sunday afternoon when Bobby leaned over and hugged his brother.

"I know you know this, but I need to say it, for my benefit if not yours. I love you, Jack, and I can't begin to tell you how relieved we all are that you are OK. I'm going to arrange to have Jackie spend several days here with you. It will take a week or so to set up, but I'll start working on it the minute I get back to Washington. I'll be back toward the end of the week. Rest and get strong. And Jack, if you need to get a message to me in the meantime, just let Sean know."

"Try to get Jackie here next weekend, Bobby. I really need to see her," Jack said. "I'll try to have her here next Friday" Bobby advised, "but one more thing Jack, please listen to me, no phone calls to anyone, I don't want anyone to know you're here, do I have your word"? "Yes, I promise" Jack replied.

With all the weeks and months he had to think things through, Bobby wasn't going to be happy to let the legal system deal with the conspirators. He'd go crazy if they got off with little or no hard time because of some fluke, a liberal-leaning judge, a conniving attorney, or a hung jury on some technicality. Bobby wanted revenge, the kind of revenge that only a corrupt mind could conjure up. He was accustomed to hearing his political enemies claim how "ruthlessly sick" he was. Those who dared to violently overthrow the president of the United States would have to pay a pound of flesh, and he would decide what part of the body it would come from. If these guys survived at all, they were going to hurt all over for the rest of their lives. He would destroy them socially, financially, and physically. These were cowards hiding behind one another, and they were going to learn they had chosen the wrong people to start a fight with. He would teach them that there are some people you just don't push too far.

Sean, recently promoted from colonel to brigadier general, had arranged for a second Special Forces team to join the team already guarding the president. Sean's command included roughly half of all the Special Forces in the U.S. military. He reported to Major General James P. Gilly, who commanded the other half of those units. They numbered some seven thousand men scattered over six bases stateside and five bases overseas. The soldiers operated in twelve-man teams, and it wasn't unusual for teams to be away "on assignment" for several weeks at a time. Even their base commanders where they were stationed, didn't know how these teams were deployed, as they answered directly to Brigadier General McDonald. Many of the teams' missions were undercover, conducted in cooperation with the CIA, so it wasn't very difficult for Sean to choose the two units he knew he could trust absolutely, and then cover their absence.

Several months before, anticipating his promotion to brigadier general, Colonel McDonald had promoted one of his closest friends from captain to major. Major Joe Santora was now commander of three Special Forces teams. Sean would choose one of these teams to be presidential protectors.

There were now twenty-four highly trained soldiers, the military's elite, guarding the president. Eight men at a time took shifts lasting three to eight hours, giving the president twenty-four-hour coverage. The eight who were off duty until the next day were able to go home to their families. It was only coincidence that both teams were from bases in Georgia, one stationed at Fort Steward about 200 miles southeast of the Wood mansion, the other at Fort Benning about 125 miles southwest. The Antonio group had arranged for hotel accommodations for the security team members at two hotels some eight miles from the Wood mansion. They had to be available at a moment's notice should the eight men on duty come under attack.

It only took four or five days for the president to regain both his mental and physical strength. He wasn't back to normal yet, but by Tuesday he was walking twice a day and starting to feel himself again. No longer feeling frail and defenseless, he began to think constructively about how he would handle his unusual situation. After all, he was still the duly elected president of the United States, regardless of what claim Jones had on that office; it was he who had been elected, not Jones. He was absolutely determined to come forward and expose what had happened to him at the hands of the conspirators.

There was a little more than three months before the November presidential election. He had been involuntarily away from American Politics since November 22. With little over 100 days to plan his return, he would not be denied his triumph. Even though the Republican convention had nominated Jones to run for president, and Jones had chosen Minnesota Senator Hubert Banfree to run as his vice president, Jack was determined to stand for reelection and have his name on the presidential ballot. He knew the majority of the people would support him, and knew he could win even if it was as a write-in candidate.

Bobby arrived back in Washington late that Sunday evening. He had little time to prepare for the number of meetings he had scheduled for Monday morning, but he was determined to spend a few hours with Jackie and fill her in on Jack's transfer from the Dallas hospital to the Wood mansion in Georgia. After landing he immediately called his sister in law. "Jackie, are you busy? I was wondering if you would like to share a cup of coffee. I have several things I'd like to talk to you about" Bobby asked. Knowing that her brother-in-law had just returned from being with Jack, Jackie jumped at the idea. "That sounds fine, I'll put a pot of coffee on right now, how long before you get here" said Jackie? "I'll be there about 9:00" Bobby responded.

Bobby went directly from the airport to Jackie's house. As the two sat down at the kitchen table, she began asking questions in rapid-fire fashion.

"Slow down, Jackie," Bobby said.

"OK, OK, just tell me all about him," she begged.

"For security reasons, I decided to move him from the hospital. He's in Georgia. Do you remember Robert Wood? "Of course I do" Jackie replied. "Jack is now a guest at his mansion. He is being guarded by Sean McDonald and a couple dozen of his heavily armed men." Bobby smiled. "He's not just OK, Jackie, he's amazingly OK. He's just as sharp as ever. He asked about you and the kids over and over again."

"Will he be all right there, Bobby?"

"He'll be just fine; don't worry about anything, Jackie. Except for the scar on his throat, you'd never know anything happened. I think when the plastic surgeons put their skills to solving that problem; no one will ever even know he had a scar there. We worked for hours bringing him up to speed on everything that has happened in the past eight months. The last thing he asked before I left was that I arrange for you to visit him next weekend. Do you feel up to it?"

"I'm ready to go the minute you say so," Jackie said.

Bobby stood up and leaned over to plant a kiss on his sister-in-law's cheek. "Well let me go, what a weekend, I'm exhausted. I'll make the arrangements and call you midweek to let you know the details, OK?"

These past eight months, Bobby had limited his contact with Jackie to short conversations every ten days or so. While she knew her husband's progress she was almost isolated from Bobby and Jack's friends, so as not to arouse any suspicion or accidentally have someone overhear something they were not supposed to hear. Jackie had longed to sit down and learn everything about Jack's progress. It had not been an easy time for the first lady, who was known for having incredible control of her demeanor. Months of being in the dark about her husband's condition left her on edge and insecure. The ordeal of witnessing her husband's attack, of moving her family out of their White House residence, of being abruptly thrust into life as a single mother, with no one to console her, had left her psychologically vulnerable. She now knew that in just a few days she would be reunited with her husband. She longed to get back to her extraordinary, normal life.

CHAPTER 10

▼

THE CONSPIRACY UNRAVELS

After arriving at the Justice Department at about seven on Monday morning, Robert Kelley stopped by his office on his way to a meeting of department heads. He was about to sit down at his desk when he saw a familiar-looking brown envelope on the seat of his chair. Before opening it, he called his secretary into his office and asked if she knew where it came from.

"I have no idea," she said. "It wasn't there on Friday afternoon when I tidied up your office and pushed the chair into the desk. I locked the office and left for the weekend right after that."

Bobby wondered who had been leaving the envelopes. This was the third one, several months after the last one.

"Whoever it is must know his or her way around government, and have access to sensitive areas. Who else could leave an envelope on the attorney general's office chair?" Bobby reasoned.

The envelope contained a hand-printed message that read, "Be careful. They are starting to watch you much more closely, and they will stop at nothing. I will be in touch very soon with much more information."

Bobby folded the note and put it in his inside jacket pocket, then picked up several manila folders and headed out to his meetings. As he passed his secretary's desk he said, "Call Dan Lockman, Shirley, and ask him to meet me in my office at three this afternoon."

Lockman was building security chief for the Justice Department. After Bobby finished his scheduled meetings, he headed back to his office to meet with him. They made small talk for a while about their families.

"How is your daughter doing in that private high school she's going to, Dan? What was the name of that school?" asked Bobby.

"St. Andrew's high school, and she's doing great. She makes the honor roll every quarter," Lockman said. "I can't thank you enough for not only getting her into St. Andrew's, but for helping pay her tuition."

"Dan, you don't have to thank me every time I ask about her. I'm happy I could help. Tell her I said hi."

"I will sir."

"I need you to do something for me Dan, quietly," Bobby went on. "I need to have a copy of the closed-circuit tapes for this floor from Friday afternoon through Monday morning. Can you do that for me?"

"I'll have the film here by 9 AM tomorrow morning," Lockman promised.

"Dan, this is to stay between you and me, OK?"

"Of course, Mr. Kelley. I understand."

Inside the beltway, politicians were abuzz with the pending release of the Werner Commission report. The commission's final report was to be released in a Rose Garden ceremony Thursday of that week. President Jones was making a big deal over the report, which he promised would put to rest the many outrageous conspiracy theories floating around over the assassination of President Kelley.

On Tuesday afternoon, with very little political wiggle room, Bobby was all but forced to attend a White House event in which President Jones signed into law one of the key pieces of legislation his brother Jack had been pushing through Congress. After signing the bill into law, Jones pulled Bobby aside and in a friendly cajoling tone told him, "I need you to be there Thursday for the release of the Werner Commission report."

Jones had set up a news conference to discuss the release of the report. Several times he had asked Bobby to attend, even when Bobby continued to politely refuse. But this time Bobby's refusal caused him to become openly hostile. In a raised voice showing just how frustrated he had become in his attempts to have a Kelley family member present at the reports release, Jones chastised,

"At a time when I am attempting to show national unity, you can't be bothered to come to such an important event?"

It was all Bobby could do to keep himself from venting his true feelings at Jones. Turning to walk away, he said, "I'm sorry Mr. President, but my schedule just doesn't permit me to attend your news conference."

"Where are you going?" Jones shot back in an intimidating voice. "I haven't dismissed you yet!"

Kelley paused, then turned around with a defiantly broad smile on his face. "Was there something else, Mr. President?"

Disgusted, Jones just threw his hands in the air. "Go on, get the hell out of here," he said.

The time to get even had not yet presented itself and Jones was after all the recognized President at this point with all the considerable power that office could direct against him. "No," Bobby thought, "this is not yet our time, but it's not far away."

Hearing reports from several casual observers of unusual travel by Attorney General Kelley, and knowing he'd been absent from his normal routine for days on end in the weeks before the release of the Werner Commission report, Jones had started to wonder if Bobby was up to something. He was unable to locate Bobby for several days when he'd tried to find him to invite him to the Werner report release ceremony.

As soon as Bobby left the room, without fully understanding why he was uneasy, Jones picked up the phone and called FBI Director Jay Howard.

"Jay, I want you to place a twenty-four-hour surveillance on Bobby Kelley," Jones ordered. "Something in the pit of my stomach is telling me something just isn't right. He's acting really strange."

"Is there something I should know, Mr. President?" Howard asked.

"No, Jay. I just have a feeling that something isn't right. I may just be paranoid with the election so close, but I want you to watch this sneaky bastard like a hawk."

The more Jones thought about it, the more he realized Kelley's normal in-your-face, sarcastic, rich-boy attitude had been different in the eight months since the assassination. Busy with his presidential duties, Jones hadn't noticed until just recently that Kelley was absent much of the time. The president then remembered that over the past several months, several of his legislative aides had complained they were unable to reach Kelley for help with legislation they were attempting to guide through Congress. Jones had never given it a second thought at the time, simply reasoning that Kelley needed time to get over the loss of his brother. But now Kelley was acting strange; he was more subdued, deferential, the way someone would act if they were hiding something.

Thankfully for the Kelley family, people in general had a great deal of sympathy for what they had gone through recently. That sympathy extended to within the ranks of the ordinary FBI agents. Bobby was at home that Tuesday evening, about to view the tapes Dan Lockman had delivered to him that morning, when the doorbell rang.

"Good evening, sir," the man outside the door said. "I'm Victor Baskin, with the FBI." After presenting his credentials, Baskin asked, "May I take a few moments of your time? I have a very important matter to discuss with you."

"Sure Agent Baskin come on in."

Inside Bobby's house, the two men stepped into the den. "Care for something to drink?" Bobby asked Baskin.

"No thank you, sir," replied Baskin.

"So what is it you want to discuss with me?" Bobby asked.

Baskin hesitated, searching for the right words to start the conversation. He had previously been part of surveillance teams monitoring congressmen and prominent businessmen. He had seen how the sensitive information he gathered about people was used to intimidate and pressure them into doing things they would not otherwise have done. He had always admired the Kelleys, and now he knew that the attorney general was being spied upon in preparation for some political pressuring.

"Mr. Kelley, I could lose my job if it's ever discovered that I came here, so I'd like your word that no one will ever learn of this meeting," Baskin said.

After Bobby assured him he would keep their meeting a secret, Baskin proceeded to tell him about the surveillance the FBI had placed on him. Bobby's first thoughts were of his brother's security.

"When did they start this surveillance?" Bobby asked.

"This afternoon."

"Not before this afternoon?"

"No, sir, I was called into the unit commander's office at four this afternoon and given orders to start surveillance of you. I asked if I was joining an existing surveillance team or initiating a new one, and the unit commander told me he had just received the order to start a new surveillance. I'm here because I do not agree with spying on a person who has given so much and is so dedicated to his country."

Bobby sighed inwardly with relief. He knew he'd been testing fate. If the surveillance had started seventy-two hours earlier, they may have discovered that Jack was still alive.

"Who gave the order for this?" Bobby asked. "It would have had to come from pretty high up."

"Who has the nerve to spy on the attorney general?" Baskin replied.

Baskin went on to say that his hands were tied; he would have to continue to shadow Bobby and file his reports as usual. He told Bobby, "I just wanted to let you know so that you would not be subjected to political blackmail if you were to do something of a highly personal nature, something you didn't want to become public knowledge. You should also know they have set up a tech team to listen in on your conversations."

As Baskin stood up to leave, he said, "I voted for your brother. The events surrounding his tragic death really affected me."

Bobby shook Baskins' hand, "thank you for letting me know about the surveillance agent Baskin, I really appreciate your kind remarks about my brother. I won't forget this, you have no idea how much this means to me and my family."

Bobby realized that someone out there was obviously getting suspicious. Knowing that his phone was tapped and that perhaps he might be followed he knew he would have to change how he communicated with Sean and the security group. They would also have to move more quickly with their plan to call a news conference to announce that Jack was still alive. Jack had been out of his coma for only four days. The pace of events was starting to quicken. In a meeting with Bobby, the Antonio group had expressed their concern that events would spiral out of control. Bobby worried that his brother wouldn't be strong enough to handle all of this.

Months before when they were discussing how the security of the convalescing president would be handled, Bobby and Sean had set up two one-word alerts they would use to signal the others that something was wrong. The alerts would only be given when they were absolutely sure a situation had come up that affected the security of the president.

The first signal was the word "Martha." Martha would be used to convey that there had been a breach in security. In such an event, a pre-designated member of the security team, one from each shift guarding the president, would be with the president constantly. It also meant that two of the three security groups would be on duty at all times, with sixteen-hour shifts, rotation of the third group every eight hours, and no trips home. Except for Sean and Bobby, all telephone communication between members of the group would cease. Only face-to-face communication between the security team members would be permitted. This would eliminate the potential of their enemies to trace phone calls via satellite. Sean or

Bobby would be in touch with the ranking officer of the team on a "must-only" basis. There could be hours or even days without further instruction.

The only food consumed by the president and his security group would be C-rations, which had been delivered to the mansion in adequate supply the day after the president arrived. They couldn't chance someone poisoning the group.

The second level of warning signal would be the word "Tiberius," a name chosen by Bobby. Tiberius was Emperor of Rome during the time of Christ. With this second warning signal, the entire security team would be required to stay at the mansion twenty-four hours a day until further notice, and the area around the mansion would be locked down. Bobby would immediately fly to Atlanta to meet with the general manager of WGST, the local affiliate of NBC. Arrangements would be made to transport the president the thirty miles to the studio for a national broadcast that would announce he was alive and expose the conspirators who attempted to assassinate him. Accompanying the president and ready to use deadly force against anyone who interfered with the transport of the president would be the entire security team in full battle gear.

Knowing the level of sophistication the government had in spying on people, and aware the FBI was listening, Bobby couldn't risk calling Sean himself, so he asked his wife to call Sean's wife and invite them for dinner and the weekend at their home on Martha's Vineyard. With clear-cut instructions on what she should say and how she should say it, Nancy placed a call to Susan McDonald. Nancy was aware that Jack was alive, but Bobby was incredibly secretive with the details of what was going on. She knew Sean's background and surmised that Sean was somehow involved in protecting her brother-in-law. She also knew that what they were doing was very dangerous and constantly asked Bobby to be careful.

"Hi Susan, it's Nancy Kelley." "Oh what a pleasant surprise" Susan responded, "Bobby asked if I would call you, He would have called Sean himself, but he's running on such a tight schedule. We were wondering if you and Sean would join us for dinner next weekend at our home on Martha's Vineyard. Be sure to tell Sean that we will pick you guys up and fly to Martha's Vineyard together. Bobby asked if you could get the dinner invitation to Sean right away and tell him that Bobby was sorry he couldn't call himself."

Susan thought this sounded a little odd, but she said, "Of course, Nancy. I'll call him right now and get back to you as soon as I talk to him. To tell you the truth, Nancy, it will do him good to get away for the weekend. He never talks about the sensitive projects he is working on, but I know he is under a lot of pressure. He seems like he's always on edge. He has never received so many calls at home from his men as he has in the past several months."

Knowing full well why Sean was on edge, Nancy interrupted Susan and cut the conversation short.

After hanging up with Nancy, Susan called her husband and told him, "I just received a call from Nancy Kelley. Bobby and Nancy just invited us to Martha's Vineyard for dinner this weekend. Nancy also wanted me to tell you that Bobby was really sorry that he was unable to call you personally, that they would pick us up and we'd fly to Martha's Vineyard together. She asked me to get the message to you right away and to call her back when I reached you."

"Martha's Vineyard is what she said, Susan?"

"Yes, Sean," Susan replied. "What in the world is going on? This whole thing sounds a little strange."

"I can't tell you right now, honey, but you will understand in the next several weeks, maybe even days," Sean said. "Call Nancy back and tell her that I did receive the message and that I'll be in touch with Bobby shortly to pick a convenient time." Sean paused, then added, "And by the way, honey, just before you called, I received word that I'm to leave immediately on a fact-finding mission for some top-secret antiterrorist project they're working on. I'll be gone several days, but I'll call you as soon as I can. Don't worry about me."

Sean immediately called Major Frank Demiani, second in command and a member of the Special Forces presidential security guard.

"Frank, it's General McDonald. I have just been asked to have dinner with Attorney General Kelley and his wife Nancy on Martha's Vineyard."

"Are you sure about that, General, Martha's Vineyard?" "Yes, Major, I'm sure," Sean answered.

"Will you be joining us any time soon, General?" "I'm on my way, Frank. You know what you have to do."

When he hung up the Major called his 2-squad leaders, "Gentlemen, I need to see you immediately and Captain Gilliam bring your entire squad with you".

As previously planned, the Werner Commission released its findings at a White House ceremony attended by a number of congressmen and senators. President Jones had invited these men in his desperate attempt to add legitimacy to the commission's controversial findings. He had tried to persuade some members of the Kelley family to attend, but each Kelley he called had some reason for not being able to make it. They all said they wanted to keep a low profile. Jones was terribly disappointed, but all he could do was graciously wish them well.

One of the congressmen invited to the ceremony was Congressman G. Michael Smith, who arrived a little early and worked his way through several small groups. Finding Jones he asked, "Mr. President, how do you think the Kelleys, especially Bobby Kelley, will react to the Werner report conclusion that a lone assassin committed the killing?"

President Jones looked around to see who might hear his reply, then shot back in a muffled voice, "I don't give a rat's ass what that son of a bitch thinks." He shook his head. "By the way, how's your brother doing?" Being from Texas, the president had known Michael's brother for decades. He was a wealthy oilman who had bankrolled Michael's campaigns for congress. He had also been a major contributor to Jones's senatorial campaigns.

"One of my aides told me you missed an intelligence meeting last week because he was in the hospital," Jones said. "I need to give him a call. Is he home yet?"

"He got out a few days ago. He's doing just fine, but I'm sure he'd like to hear from you."

"By the way," Smith continued, "I bumped into Bobby Kelley one evening when I was leaving the hospital after visiting my brother. He said he was there to visit a close friend of his family, a cousin or something."

Jones immediately pulled Smith by his arm and walked together several feet until they were alone, the president pulling Michael's jacket lapels so close they were pressing up against each other.

"What's wrong Mr. President?" the congressman asked. "Which hospital did you see Kelley going into?"

"It was Parkland Memorial."

"You saw Bobby Kelley entering Parkland Memorial Hospital in Dallas a week ago?" Jones asked incredulously.

"Yes, Mr. President. It was last Friday night. Is something wrong, Mr. President?"

"I'm not sure, Michael, but I'll let you know," Jones replied, a sick feeling growing in the pit of his stomach. "I just knew Kelley was up to something," he thought. "I'll bet he is planning some sort of devious election surprise, but why Dallas?"

President Jones began making his way out of the room, stopping only two or three times to speak briefly to some of the dignitaries he had invited. Back in the Oval Office, he placed a call to FBI Director Howard.

"Jay, do you know that Bobby Kelley was seen entering Parkland Memorial Hospital last week to visit a close relative? Has your surveillance on Bobby Kelley turned up anything out of the ordinary," asked Jones? "I want to know who he was visiting, and Jay I need to know ASAP. Why would a close family member of the Kelleys be in a Dallas hospital? They're from Hyannis and Boston. Something is going on, Jay, and I need to know. Put your best people on this and get back to me."

Within hours FBI lawyers were in court before a federal judge with a motion to subpoena the hospital records of Parkland Memorial. Armed with the subpoena, four senior FBI agents were on their way to Dallas in an FBI Learjet by six the next morning. They'd land about eight that morning and had all day Friday but would spend the entire weekend if necessary to get to the bottom of this. Upon arriving at the hospital, they asked to see the hospital administrator and presented him with the subpoena. The administrator picked up the phone and called his assistant to come to his office.

"Brian I have some federal agents here in my office. I need to see you right away." It only took Brian Neville about a minute and a half to get to his boss's office. Once he was there, his boss told him, "Brian, these men are with the FBI. They have served us with a subpoena to inspect our records. I want you to cooperate in every way and to accompany these men to make sure all the hospital employees cooperate in helping them retrieve whatever they need."

As they made their way to the records and computer room, the senior agent informed Neville that they were specifically looking for members of former president Kelley's immediate family who might have been admitted to the hospital within the past several months.

Neville told the agents, "I seriously doubt that a member of Kelley's family could have been admitted to the hospital without me knowing about it."

The agents further explained that the patient was in the hospital last Friday and was either still there or was discharged within the last week. As the five men entered the computer room, Neville said, "I don't know how something like that could have gotten past me, but we'll start with a list of recent discharges."

One of the hospital's tech managers made a printout of the names and addresses of several hundred current and recently discharged patients. Culling through the names the agents found none on the list were named Kelley. Next they checked the date of admission. They had only been at it for four hours when one of the agents asked why a patient would have been in the hospital eight months for a stroke and brain surgery. The question got the attention of the other three agents. They began reading the lengthy medical reports of Mr. Michael Reardon, who was admitted into the emergency room November 22 of last year with a severe head wound. The record was later changed to read "stroke with brain damage requiring brain surgery." He had been discharged last Friday, exactly one week ago.

One of the agents asked Neville, "Are any of the doctors who treated Mr. Reardon on duty now?"

Neville looked at the list of doctors who had treated Reardon. He called the ER and asked, "Who am I speaking with,". "This is Mary Evan" the nurse answered. "This is Brian Neville Mary, I need to know if doctors Jordan, Bailey, or Azar are on duty right now."

"Dr. Jordan is here," the nurse said. "But he is with a patient."

When Neville told the agents that Doctor Bill Jordan was on duty as we speak, the agents immediately got up and asked Neville to escort them to the emergency room. When they arrived the agents told Neville to find another doctor take over for Dr. Jordan. Neville explained to Dr. Jordan that the agents had some questions for him.

"Are you the same doctor who treated a Mr. Reardon?" one of the agents asked.

"That name sounds familiar," Dr. Jordan replied.

Showing the doctor Reardon's medical charts, the agent asked, "doctor are these your signatures signing off on various treatments for Reardon?"

Knowing who Mike Reardon was, Jordan sensed immediately that he was in big trouble. "Look," he said, "I was only part of a team of doctors and nurses that treated Reardon. What is this all about? Is there something wrong? Is Mr. Reardon OK?" The doctor seemed to be getting agitated. "Let me say something up front," he continued. "if you want to question me about the treatment I rendered to a patient I'm not going to leave myself wide open for a possible malpractice suit. If you intend to question me about the treatment of any patient, I want my attorney present."

The agents refused to give Dr. Jordan the privilege of calling his attorney. They insisted that he follow them into a private room to resume questioning, but Jordan refused. The agents threatened him with arrest, but he still refused to discuss the Reardon case without the presence of his attorney.

Dr. Jordan asked one of the nurses "would you please call security and have them contact the Dallas Police. "These men are threatening to arrest me, but they don't even have an arrest warrant," he said. "Gentlemen, I absolutely refuse to answer any more questions without my attorney present. Let me caution you, there are a number of witnesses to your strong arm intimidation and refusal of my constitutional rights."

Also in the emergency room that Friday afternoon were two members of the team that had treated Reardon, one of them a doctor and one a nurse named Judy Drummed. Drummed overheard Neville telling Jordan "what's the big deal Bill, "answer their questions about Reardon and be done with it." She also heard Jordan say to Neville, "Look, Brian, I have nothing to hide, but I'm not going to discuss the treatment of one of my patients with law enforcement officers without having my lawyer present, period." Instinctively Drummed knew the men who were questioning Dr. Jordan were federal agents. From what she heard them saying, they may not have put all the pieces together yet about Reardon, but they seemed to be dangerously close to figuring out who Reardon really was.

Drummed calmly walked to the break room, telling her coworker on the way that she would be right back. Months before, each member of President Kelley's medical team had been given Kenny O'Donnell's private telephone number so they could call him with any news about the president's condition. Drummed knew she had to let O'Donnell know what was happening. She was part of the team of medical professionals who worked on the President. She knew the whole story. She now sensed Dr. Jordan was in big trouble and could be arrested. Someone close to the Kelleys needed to know these federal agents were snooping around.

After the assassination, at the insistence of the President Jones, O'Donnell had stayed on the job as special assistant to the president. He often received calls about Jack's condition while standing just a few yards from the man they all suspected of being one of the assassination conspirators. The call from Judy Drummed came in just as O'Donnell was about to go into a special meeting with President Jones; FBI Director Howard; Congressman G. Michael Smith, chairman of the house committee on intelligence; Senator Bill Doakes, chairman of the Senate intelligence committee; and Attorney General Kelley. The purpose of the meeting was to discuss several credible threats of a new round of terrorist activities in the aftermath of the 9/11 terrorist attacks in New York and Washington.

"Mr. O'Donnell, this is Judy Drummed, do you remember me? "Yes of course I do Judy", O'Donnell said. "I know you may not be able to respond to everything I am about to tell you," Drummed told O'Donnell, "so just listen so I can get this out before either of us are interrupted."

It was about 2:15 PM Dallas time (3:15 Washington time) as Drummed explained, "Four men who look like FBI agents are in the hospital questioning Dr. Jordan about Mr. Reardon's medical file. I can tell they haven't connected all the pieces together yet, but it won't be long before they do. From the best I can tell, Dr. Jordan wasn't telling them anything, but they are threatening to arrest him. I have to go now, but I'll call you back when I learn anything else"

O'Donnell thanked her for the call. "I'll pass everything on and call you back later," he said. "I am about to go into a meeting with the president, but I'll be sure to pass that information along to our friends."

On his way into the Oval Office meeting, Bobby Kelley deliberately walked a few yards out of his way to go by O'Donnell's office. As he stuck his head in the door to say hello before going into the meeting, O'Donnell asked him to come in and close the door behind him.

"I just received a call from a nurse named Judy Drummed. She is one of the nurses who worked on Jack. She told me that there are four federal agents in Parkland Hospital questioning one of the ER doctors, a Dr. Jordan, about the medical file of Michael Reardon."

Bobby had met Dr. Jordan just last Friday. Jordan had been there when Dr. Clark walked the president out of the hospital for his trip to Atlanta. Bobby leapt to his feet.

"Oh my God, Kenny, they know! I can't go into this meeting. I can't concentrate on anything except to get to Jack. Kenny, tell them that I became violently ill and was vomiting all over the place. I have to get with Sean and Jack and let them know that they are on the verge of discovering everything. How in the world did they find out?"

Events were moving very fast. It was Friday afternoon, only a week since they had moved Jack from Dallas and three days since he had given the security team the "Martha Vineyard" coded warning. Now he was about to throw caution to the wind and call Sean with the warning "Tiberius." He was full of doubt and hoped he wasn't overreacting. Did he really have to expose Jack to this much stress? He knew Jack wasn't as strong as they had originally wanted him to be, but if they didn't act now, it could mean that his brother and a number of others, including him, would die.

Bobby knew that by calling Sean direct on his cell phone, he was running the risk the enemy would trace his call and be on top of the president before he could pull off his plan. He knew he was being watched and listened to very closely, but he had no choice, he had to error on the side of caution. Events were moving faster than he could control, and he had to do whatever he could to protect his brother. Leaving the White House, he decided he'd stop at a pay phone to call Sean rather than use his cell phone. It would take a little longer to trace such a call. Besides, they wouldn't fully understand what he meant by "Tiberius." He would call and arrange a flight and be in Atlanta in two hours.

It would only be a matter of hours before the FBI agents at the hospital would report to their superiors that there was no record of a Kelley family member being admitted to or treated at Parkland Hospital. When they further explained that a person named Reardon was admitted on November 22, that he was originally admitted with a gunshot wound to the head, and that they were unable to locate him, it would be impossible not to connect the dots. Add to this the report that Bobby Kelley had been in Dallas visiting a relative at Parkland Hospital, and they'd know. These conspirators were anything but dopes.

Calling from a pay phone at the side of the road, Bobby reached Sean as he was on his way from the Peachtree Dekalb Airport to the mansion. Bobby was ecstatic and relieved that he reached Sean on the first try. At least now Jack would have substantially heightened security.

"Sean, I can't go into very much detail, but that Tiberius guy is not very far away," Bobby said. "I was just in the White House moments ago, They know our friend Tiberius. Sean, follow the plan exactly as we set it up. I am on my way to the peoples station, (rather than actually name the TV station they had prear-ranged to call WGST the peoples station), I will be there in about two hours. Please have our friend there ready to go on at our synchronized time plus my travel time. Be careful and God Bless!"

Sean McDonald simply replied, "OK, Bobby."

When the meeting at the White House convened, President Jones asked O'Donnell if he knew where the attorney general had gone to. O'Donnell explained that he had in fact talked to the attorney general just moments before the meeting and that the attorney general had been vomiting profusely.

"In fact, he was on his way here when he lost control. He was unable to hold anything down. He realized he was in no shape to come to this meeting."

About a quarter of the way through the meeting, the president's phone rang. The president excused himself and went into another room to take the call, then rejoined the meeting without saying a word. He had just taken his seat when there was another interruption. This time it was Howard's phone ringing. such interruptions were highly unusual at presidential meetings but Director Howard had warned the president that his agents in Dallas might interrupt the meeting. They had called their office to report what they had found at the hospital, and now they wanted to report directly to Howard on the matter, which was impor-tant enough to warrant interrupting their boss in his meeting with the president.

The director took the call in front of the others. He listened intently as his agents explained all they had found. He asked, "Have you tracked down this Reardon person? Do you know where he lives?"

Sitting just a few feet away, O'Donnell, who had not been paying attention to the Director or what he was saying, nearly jerked his head turning to look at Howard when he said the name Reardon. He then realized the president was looking at him and that he had inadvertently given himself away. Jones didn't yet know anything about Reardon, but he now knew that O'Donnell did.

"The address on Reardon's hospital records is no longer a viable address," Howard's agent said over the phone. "We found out that the area had been part of a huge urban renewal project and that they tore down the whole area over a year ago."

"And you are sure that a member of the Kelley family was not admitted to or treated at the hospital?" Howard asked.

"Yes, sir."

"Well done. Wrap up your investigation, and be sure to take with you copies of all pertinent documents. Report to me first thing Monday morning," Howard ordered. He hung up the phone and sat down with a puzzled look on his face. Then he looked at Smith and said, "Congressman Smith, are you absolutely sure you ran into Bobby Kelley last Friday night at a hospital in Dallas?"

Smith was taken aback. Looking at the president while addressing the FBI director, Smith said, "Who told you that I saw Bobby Kelley last Friday night?"

"That's not important, congressman. Did you see Kelley going into a Dallas hospital last Friday?" Howard wanted to know?

"I asked you a question, Mr. Howard. Who told you that I saw Bobby Kelley in Dallas last week?" Smith repeated.

Howard's face was blank. He acted like he hadn't heard the question.

Smith turned toward the president and said, "Mr. President, what in the world is going on?"

O'Donnell sat there listening to the exchange between Congressman Smith and Jay Howard. Smith was furious. He knew the casual comment he had made to Jones just a few days before must have been repeated to Director Howard. "Mr. President, what would cause the FBI to investigate an innocent encounter with Bobby Kelley at a hospital? What is going on here?" Smith asked Jones.

"I don't like the tone of your voice, congressman. Get hold of your attitude and your tongue!" Jones said as he leaned forward, starting to show his annoyance.

"So you did see Kelley going into the hospital?" Howard piped in.

"Go to hell, Howard," Smith said, his face now showing his anger at the whole conversation. "Look, I know you guys have a long-running feud with the Kelleys. I did like Jack Kelley, rest his soul, but I am not what one would consider a great fan of Bobby Kelley. But until you people tell me what is going on here, I refuse to be part of any witch-hunt targeting the Kelleys. What could be so important about me bumping into Robert Kelley in Dallas? Mr. President, it is obvious that this meeting has ended. Have a good weekend!" With that Smith got up and left the room. But Jones was too anxious to find out who Michael Reardon was to worry about Smith leaving the room.

As O'Donnell began to gather the files he had brought into the meeting, the president said, "Kenny can you stay a few minutes....I have something I want to discuss with you."

Director Howard was also leaving, so the president got up and walked him to the door. "Jay," President Jones whispered, "I want you to put people on everyone who has anything to do with the Kelleys. The call I took during the meeting was from DIA. Their comfort level regarding someone called Brigadier General Sean McDonald is causing DIA Intelligence some concern. It seems he and Bobby Kelley have been scheming about something. I want to know everything about this General McDonald, especially everything he has been doing in the past year. Phone records, travel records, everything. Call me this weekend. And who is this Reardon guy your agents talked to you about. O'Donnell recognized the name."

"I'm not sure yet, Mr. President. I'll call you after reading the report."

When everyone had left the room, Jones asked O'Donnell, "What do you know about this Dallas thing?"

"What do you mean, Mr. President? What Dallas thing?" "You know, Kenny. You're good friends with the Kelleys. Why all the secrecy, what's going on?"

"What's going on about what, sir?"

"About Bobby being in Dallas claiming he was there visiting a close relative at Parkland Hospital. Who is Michael Reardon, Kenny?"

Before Kenny could answer, Jones said, "the reason I excused myself to take that call a little while ago was because it had to do with some information I received about General McDonald. I asked DIA to have your phone records pulled."

"Why are you pulling my phone records, Mr. President?" Kenny's voice changed as he started to lose his temper. "What the hell are you so suspicious about, sir? I've served you well since you became president. You have no right to violate my privacy."

"Kenny, why all of a sudden are you so friendly with a General McDonald who coincidentally heads up much of the command of the U.S. Special Forces?" Jones asked.

"Mr. President, what do you mean all of a sudden, I've known Sean McDonald for more than twenty years. We went to Harvard together. Over the years we have often dined with our wives".

Jones leaned over his desk and said, in a gentler voice, "Look Kenny, you've done a good job of making the transition between Jack Kelley's administration and mine. I know you go way back with the Kelleys. I also know that there is something going on. If Bobby Kelley is being so secretive about something, it can't be good for me. I've known all of you long enough to understand that when it comes to the Kelleys, Kenny O'Donnell is always in the loop. So what's going on Kenny? You know I'm going to get to the bottom of this, and if you screw me, Kenny, you know me well enough that I *will* get even. I don't want to have that kind of relationship with you. So just tell me what Bobby is up to. Who is this Reardon character?"

Kenny insisted he didn't know what was happening as he stood up and started walking toward the door.

"Mr. President, you need to find yourself a new chief of staff. I quit. I've had enough of this for one day, may I be excused," as he opened the door, not waiting for the presidents response.

CHAPTER 11

▼

MY FELLOW AMERICANS

On his way to the airport for his flight to Atlanta, Bobby called the first lady to let her know that the plans for her to visit Jack would have to be postponed. He wasn't worried about the FBI listening to his phone call. Even if the FBI surveillance team picked up every word he said, they probably wouldn't submit any of it until the end of their shift.

"I'm sorry, I don't have much I can tell you at this point," Bobby said to Jackie. "Our plans have changed. I'm on my way to help the president make his address to the nation. Events have forced us to do this sooner than we might have wanted to, but everything is OK, Jackie. Turn on your TV and watch what happens. We will be sending for you to join us later on this evening. Pack a light bag, OK. I've got to run. Sorry I can't tell you more at this point, but I can tell you it's all about to come together for us."

"Bobby, he is OK, isn't he?" Jackie said, wanting some reassurance.

"He's fine, Jackie! Turn your TV on. In a few hours you'll see for yourself," Bobby reassured.

A half-hour outside Hartsfield International, Bobby called Joe Samere, a long-time friend of his who was now the general manager of WGST. The Antonio group had done their homework and planned this months before. Joe Samere had graduated from Harvard Law School a year ahead of Bobby, Sean, and Kenny. Samere's secretary took the call, thinking it was one of her boss's prankster buddies when she asked who was calling; the person on the other end of the line identified himself as "Attorney General Robert Kelley." Samere had a group of friends who were constantly pulling pranks on each other. On Samere's fortieth birthday one of them had a truckload of chicken manure dumped on his front lawn. It stank up the neighborhood for days before being removed.

When Samere picked up the phone he recognized Bobby's voice and immediately knew it was no joke. "Joe how are you" Bobby asked? "Great Bobby, how are you? Its' been years, but I read about you all the time" Samere offered.

"I'm fine Joe but I need you to do something for me, Joe, as quickly as possible," Bobby said. "I need it to be done in such a way that most of your preparation is done in secret over the next several minutes. Can you arrange to have a studio ready so that I can make a broadcast to the entire nation? Can you do that with only your closest assistants so that at least for the next thirty minutes, no one knows it's being prepared for me? This is of national importance, Joe."

Samere couldn't believe what he was hearing. "I just can't turn over a studio and give you access to a national audience without knowing more about what this is all about."

"I need to trust you with keeping a secret for the next thirty or forty-five minutes. Can you do that for me? By secret I mean that you can be the only person who knows what this is about."

"What *is* this all about, Bobby?" Samere asked once again?

"Can you keep this a secret, Joe?" Bobby asked. When Samere promised he would, Bobby told him, "The reason I need to go on national TV has to do with my brother's assassination."

"What about your brother's assassination, Bobby?"

"He's alive, Joe," Bobby said.

"Are you serious, Bobby? Is this some sort of a sick joke?" Samere's voice elevating as he couldn't believe what he was hearing.

"Do you think I would make something like that up, Joe?" Bobby shot back. "He is not only alive Joe, he is on his way to your studios as we speak. He is traveling with several dozen heavily armed members of our Special Forces. My brother wants to use your studio to speak to the nation and announce that he is alive and will shortly expose the conspirators who tried to kill him."

"Bobby, you are serious, aren't you? I stand ready to do whatever the president requires of me. I'll not only have the studio ready for the president, I will make some phone calls to our New York affiliates to make sure the national networks are ready to cut into regular programming for the Presidents speech. I won't tell them anything about the president until he arrives in the building."

"Joe, in about a half hour I want you to leak to the press that the president of the United States is about to make a major announcement regarding the Kelley assassination," Bobby said. "The address to the nation by my brother should be fed into all major broadcast media. No reporters will be allowed anywhere near the president. In fact, if they get too pushy, our security people will be quite rough with them. They should know this up front and understand that the president's assassins are for the most part still capable of trying to kill him. The soldiers protecting the president will have no tolerance for even the slightest interference."

Next, Bobby called Atlanta Police Commissioner Jim Day. Robert Wood, who had considerable influence with the police commissioner, had already spoken to Day to prepare him for Bobby's call. Bobby knew his brother and Sean would need the cooperation of the Atlanta Police, so during the flight to Atlanta he had called Wood to ask if he would use his influence to convince Commissioner Day to fully cooperate with him.

"Commissioner Day, it's Attorney General Robert Kelley calling," Bobby began. "I'm calling because I need your help in a vital security matter." "Nice to hear from you sir, how can I help". Day immediately offered his services without knowing what any of this was about.

"Commissioner Day," Bobby continued, "can your men clear a path for the president of the United States? He will be entering the downtown area off Highway 85 on Spring Street and will be going to WGST studios on West Peachtree Street to give an emergency address to the nation. If you could arrange to have the traffic yield to his motorcade, that would be appreciated. I realize this is short notice, but he will be coming down 85 in the next fifteen minutes or so."

"As soon as we hang up, Mr. Kelley, I'll have four or five motorcycle officers join up with the president's motorcade along 85 and several more along the route to ensure the president has a clean shot from the highway to the studio," Day replied. "Is there anything else I can do, sir?"

"There is one more thing," Bobby said. "I'm due to arrive at Hartsfield in about fifteen or twenty minutes. If I could have a police escort from the airport to the WGST studio to join the President, it would be greatly appreciated." Commissioner Day told Bobby he would have his requests acted upon immediately. Bobby never told him which president was coming, and of course President Jones was the only man they would be expecting. Everyone knew President Kelley had been assassinated.

Upon arriving at the airport, Bobby Kelley instructed the police captain who greeted him to have several of his officers guard his plane.

"Under no circumstances should anyone get near the plane, regardless of who it is," Bobby instructed, knowing full well the plane would be their exit from the Atlanta area. Bobby gave the officer his cell-phone number and instructed him to call should anyone attempt to gain access to the plane.

Leaving the Oval Office meeting, Kenny too had had the sense it would only be a matter of hours before their enemies connected the dots and realized that they had botched the assassination. Kenny left the White House and called Bobby from a pay phone a few blocks away.

"Bobby, I just had the most incredible meeting of my life. I can't talk about it now except to say that you're right, they are right on top of finding out about everything. They know about Sean, so be careful not to call him on his cell, or they'll know where he is. Where are you now Bobby?"

"I'm on my way to the people's station," Bobby responded. Kenny knew exactly what that meant.

Just before he hung up, Kenny asked, "Have you thought about having several of Sean's men stationed at Jackie's home? It wouldn't be a bad idea to cover your house and mine also. You never know what form revenge will take when these guys realize they're cornered. They have proved they are capable of almost anything."

"I'll tell Sean, Kenny. I'll be with him in little less than half an hour."

O'Donnell then called his wife. "Mary, thank God you're home. Please cancel everything that's going on this weekend. We need to batten down the hatches for the next few days. Some very serious stuff is about to happen. Get the kids back home from wherever they are."

"I just heard announced on the radio that the president will address the nation in about thirty minutes about major developments in the Kelley assassination. What's going on, Kenny? Should I be worried?"

"I'm on my way home. I'll be there in ten or fifteen minutes. I'll explain everything when I get there. Don't worry, honey. Everything will be fine."

Kenny assured her. As if it was an afterthought Mary told Kenny, "By the way honey, about forty-five minutes ago this military jeep pulled up in front of the house with four uniformed soldiers carrying rifles. They're still there, two sitting in the jeep and two standing outside of it. Are we in any danger, Kenny?"

"No, honey, we're not. I'll be right there."

After O'Donnell and Director Howard left the Oval Office meeting, President Jones asked Janet, his secretary, to make sure he was not disturbed. He had several very sensitive phone calls to make to line up votes for some upcoming legislation, Completely unaware that the country was getting ready to hear a presidential address, President Jones had been cleaning up a number of things before retreating to Camp David for the weekend. His secretary had received several phone calls from people asking about the up coming presidential address. Recognizing the announced airtime was approaching, she began to wonder why none of the usual preparations, with assistants and makeup and the like, were being made.

Janet knocked on the door of the Oval Office and stepped inside.

"Are you ready for your address to the nation, Mr. President?" she asked.

"What address to the nation?"

"It's all over the radio and TV, Mr. President. You're supposed to be addressing the nation about major developments in the Kelley assassination."

"What are you talking about, Janet?"

Jones stood up and walked across the room to turn on two of the three television sets in his office. Lo and behold, the talking heads were all abuzz speculating about what kinds of developments the president would be talking about. Jones was incredulous. He walked back to his desk to make some phone calls and to try to find out what in the hell was going on.

When Robert Wood learned that the president was about to travel downtown to deliver a nationally televised speech to the nation, he insisted that the president travel in his personal limousine, which was specially equipped and modified with bulletproof glass and steel plates. The military security force had five SUVs for transporting the small contingent of Special Forces. As they entered the highway for the trip to downtown Atlanta, they formed a blockade around the president's limo. They drove in front of, behind, and on each side of the limo, and would not allow any other vehicle to get near it.

The trip downtown took thirty minutes. As they entered the downtown area known as the connector, several motorcycle police officers waiting alongside the highway pulled in front of the motorcade and began escorting it to the studios, as requested. The police had also blocked off traffic to give the president a clear path for the four blocks from the highway to the studios. As the president's limo pulled up in front of the studios, the members of the security force jumped out of their vehicles and quickly secured the entrance leading to the WGST offices.

It was a Friday afternoon in downtown Atlanta, and with all the commotion of police barricades being set up and the heightened presence of police security, several dozen office workers and pedestrians had begun to linger behind the police line asking what was going on.

When the motorcade pulled up in front of the WGST office building and the president stepped out of the car, dozens of people across the street recognized who he was. They were stunned to silence; they couldn't believe their eyes. A hush fell over the crowd there was total disbelief! How could this be? Was it really him? One man could be heard mumbling, "That guy looks just like President Kelley." A collective gasp rose up from the small crowd. Seconds seemed like minutes as their minds tried to make sense of what they were seeing. And then, as if to accept the reality, they spontaneously began clapping, shouting, "God bless you, Mr. President!"

Hearing this, President Kelley paused briefly. He raised his arm and with two fingers in the form of a V, waved to the crowd across the street acknowledging their applause.

Police Commissioner Day, who was on hand to make sure all went well with the presidential visit, had been expecting President Jones. The sight of President Kelley emerging from the limo caught him completely off guard. His eyes welled up as he shook hands with the president he had thought was dead. President Kelley, who looked good in whatever he wore, was wearing a dark pinstriped business suit; except for seeming a little tired, he looked great.

"I am overjoyed to see you, sir," Day said.

"Jim, you have no idea how overjoyed I am to be seen. Thank you for your help in securing our visit. I really do appreciate everything you've done." The president was quickly escorted into the WGST offices and directly to the TV studio, where he immediately recognized Joe Samere.

"Thank you, Joe," the president said, approaching Samere to shake his hand. "I really appreciate what you are doing."

Understanding the importance of getting this man in front of the cameras, Samere motioned the president to follow him. He led the way into the studio and sat Jack down at a desk before the cameras. Joi Cerrito, a local hairdresser and makeup artist who contracted with WGST, spent several moments clipping and fixing the president's hair, and bringing some color to his ash-white skin. Months of being indoor as well as the ordeal he had been through was obvious in his weary look and ash white complexion. Within a few minutes, Joi had the president looking fit, well groomed, and tanned.

Samere signaled the producer and an announcer proclaimed, "The programs normally seen at this time have been temporarily postponed to bring you this special announcement from the president of the United States." Then the cameras switched to the president as he began his address.

In the Oval Office, still making phone calls trying to find out what was going on, President Jones's jaw dropped when he saw Jack Kelley appear on his TV screen. He couldn't believe his eyes as he walked across his office to draw closer to the televisions and turn up the sound.

"My fellow Americans, this is not a hoax. I am in fact John Francis Kelley, President of the United States. What I am about to reveal to you is a terrifying but true story. On November 22 of last year, months of planning by a group of conspirators culminated in my attempted murder. From the time the bullets struck me at 12:30 PM Dallas time on November 22, until approximately one week ago, I lay in an unconscious state. I am here today thanks to friends and trusted aides who quickly realized that a major breach in security had allowed assassins to attempt to kill me. In their efforts to protect me from further attempts on my life, my friends covered up the fact that while I was very seriously wounded, I was not dead.

I was attended to by a courageous group of medical professionals, guarded by a fearless group of the U.S. military Special Forces, and provided for by friends and close relatives. In the hours and days immediately after my attempted murder, only two or three people thought I could survive such serious wounds. These people never gave up. All of them knew that standing up against the men who perpetrated this act could have cost them their own lives. To these friends: I intend to thank each of you more formally in the weeks ahead, but for now let me say thank you from the bottom of my heart."

As the president continued his address, Bobby arrived in the studio and made his way to the sound room just off the studio his brother was speaking from. His eyes met Jack's, and they both immediately knew they had a mutual feeling of completion; they were once again a team. It had been an unbelievable journey for both of these men, and they were now about to expose the evil that had nearly cost them everything.

"It is no small miracle," the president continued, "that I am here before you this afternoon. I would have preferred to have another week or two to continue regaining my strength, but my enemies were very close to finding out that they botched my assassination. They would have stopped at nothing to silence me. They would have killed everyone around me. So with a little levity in the face of such hostility and evil, I can report that much to the chagrin of these conspirators, the reports of my demise have been greatly exaggerated. I stand here before you today weak, but anxious to expose those responsible for the attempted takeover of our country, and anxious to resume my duties as your president.

"The people of this country, backed by proud heritage, abundant resources, and their own skills and intelligence, are fully capable of sustaining this republic and living in freedom. We have endured many serious tests of our form of representative government over these two-hundred-plus years. And we will as a people, bound together by a common goal, survive this as well. True democratic values do not breed murderous ideologies. We are a nation founded on the rule of law. True democracies encourage the peaceful pursuit of a better life so their citizens can fully share in the progress of our times. Our nation has for decades inspired other nations of the world. The act of murdering a leader, duly elected by the people, nearly succeeded. When the people of our nation disagree with an elected official, they don't murder him. They simply wait until the next election and vote him out of office.

"Parties loyal to our cause have been quietly investigating the assassination and its cover-up from the days after the shots were fired. Having been briefed on their findings, I am here to tell you that those who conspired to murder me and take over our country include politicians from the highest offices in our government. They include military officers in the highest ranks at the Pentagon. They include chief executives of Fortune 500 companies. These groups conspired to enlist members of Mafia crime families to do their dirty work for payment of one million dollars".

"Mind you, it wasn't money the Mafia was interested in it was revenge. My administration has indicted their bosses for many criminal activities. We are still investigating how these groups came together to organize and execute this attempted coup d'e.tat. I will, in the weeks ahead, continue to report to you our findings on these matters.

"I intend to expose the current occupant of the White House, sworn in under circumstances he himself helped to create. In the fullness of time, we intend to expose how he was central to the cover-up of the facts surrounding my attempted assassination. I intend to show the Werner Commission's wanton disregard for investigating facts surrounding this conspiracy and the secrecy with which they did so. With the commission's members including a chief justice of the Supreme Court, two congressmen, two senators, a former CIA director, and the president of the World Bank, it will only be a matter of time before their culpability in this conspiracy becomes public knowledge. Those of us who despise the evil one man can inflict upon another will be outraged that many we have completely trusted have conspired against us, behind the scenes.

"I intend to expose the military officers who, in conjunction with the CEOs of billion-dollar defense contractors, played a key role in the assassination and its cover-up. And finally I intend to name names and point fingers at the members of organized crime families who joined the others to kill me out of revenge. I pledge that I will hunt down these people wherever they hide and bring them to justice. I am today announcing that the attorney general has convened a grand jury. Late this afternoon, subpoenas will be served on Pentagon officials, certain members of the FBI, and each member of the Werner Commission to testify about what they knew regarding this conspiracy.

"Until I have fully regained my strength and have exposed each of those involved in this coup d'e.tat, I will make my home base known only to a select few. From there I will be able to secure both my safety and the safety of my family. I will continue to keep you informed about these matters. Thank you for your support, and may God bless America!"

It was a warm Friday afternoon, one of the last weekends of summer. Labor day weekend was a few weeks away and next week would once again be a short workweek as many in Washington took vacation days to give them 3 or 4-day weekends. Most of the White House staff had left work early to beat the traffic and get a jump on their weekend activities. All alone in the Oval Office, his wife and daughters back in Texas on the family ranch, Jones sat staring at the television screen in disbelief, hanging on to President Kelley's every word. Jones was totally blindsided by the reemergence of Jack Kelley. His body began to quiver, and then quickly developed into uncontrollable shaking. He had no clue how all of this was happening.

His mind bolted from one thing to another. "They had planned this so thoroughly," Jones thought. "They assured me they had all the bases covered. How could Jack Kelley still be alive?"

This past year Jones had had fantasies about his exalted place in American history. He was convinced he would go down in history as one of the great presidents. He guided major pieces of legislation through Congress and changed the course of history with regard to the rights of minorities. Now he realized he would go down in history as a traitor, a conspirator. He was disgraced and confused about what to do next. How would he ever face his wife and daughters? His life's work was destroyed. In his thirty years in government he had held some of the highest offices in the land. He had lifted himself out of poverty to become a multimillionaire and the leader of the most powerful nation humankind has ever known.

How was it to end? Would he spend the rest of his life in prison, or worse, be put to death himself? The trial he would face would be humiliating. He had appointed hundreds of judges in his career, and he would now be dragged before one of them as a common criminal, handcuffed with leg shackles, to be tried for murder and treason. Jones walked across the room to his desk. He stood in front of it and began staring stoically through the window at the Washington Monument. He picked up the phone to call his wife. When she answered he simply said, "You know I have always loved you. I'm sorry. I never thought it would come to this. Kiss the girls for me, and tell them I love them."

"Lincoln! Lincoln, listen to me!" Mrs. Jones cried, trying to keep her husband on the line. She was still talking when he hung up the phone.

Contemplating what he would do next, his phones ringing one after the other, Jones walked behind his desk, opened the top drawer, and removed a .32 caliber Berretta handgun. The shaking nearly stopped as he thought about what he was about to do. A feeling of calm came over him. He sat down in his chair behind the desk that so many other presidents had sat behind. Setting the gun down on the desk, he picked up a pen and scrawled on a piece of paper the words "I'm sorry. This was not what I wanted." Staring across the room as if in a daze, the televisions still abuzz with the story about President Kelley, his body now relaxed and no longer shaking, Jones put the barrel of the gun in his mouth and pulled the trigger.

After thanking Joe Samere and his staff of television personnel for helping him get his message out to the nation, President Kelley left for his trip to the airport to board the plane that would take him to his family compound, where he would be reunited with his wife and children. On his way out he stopped to have a word with General McDonald.

"Sean, my safety continues to be in your capable hands. Will you have any problems defending us at my family compound?"

"Mr. President," Sean replied, "I don't think you're in as much danger now as you were before that speech. These guys will now be on the run. and I don't believe they have the stomach to stand up and try to shore up this conspiracy. People like that operate behind the scenes, and you have just opened the curtains in their dark room and exposed them to the sunlight. We won't let our guard down for a second, but I don't believe these guys are as much a threat as they were an hour ago."

President Kelley left the studios and headed for the airport with his brother and the large contingent of security people. It would take about two and a half hours by air and about a half hour by ground to reach the compound. Arrangements had to be made in advance of their arrival. They needed transportation from the airport, and they would need a huge delivery of food. There weren't that many places to eat in town, and certainly not enough hotel rooms to house so many people. For a while anyway, they'd all have to stay at the compound.

As the plane reached its cruising altitude of 21,000 feet, news of President Jones's suicide reached the cockpit. The pilot turned over controls to his copilot and got up to tell the president the tragic news. "Mr. President, I have just heard news that President Jones has committed suicide."

"That son of a bitch," Bobby blurted out without hesitation, from his seat next to Jack. "I always knew he was a coward."

Sean turned to Bobby and said, "This is a turn of events we could not have planned for."

"Sean is right," Jack said to Bobby. "With Jones gone that whole group will probably run like dogs."

Bobby nodded. "You're probably right Jack, all but the Italians, they won't run. We are going to have to deal with them differently than we deal with the others. Leave them to me, Jack. I have an idea on how to deal with them in the only way they will understand."

Jack leaned closer to his brother and said, "Maybe we are being too defensive. Maybe we need to go on offense and go to Washington instead of the compound." Motioning to one of the security people, Jack asked to have the general join him.

"Yes, Mr. President?" Sean said.

"Have a seat, Sean. Bobby and I would like to bounce some security questions off you and see what you think about changing some of our plans."

President Kelley began to lay out a bold plan for going directly back to the White House. "Correct me if I'm wrong Sean, but to hell with these guys. Wouldn't we all be a whole lot more secure at the White House? With its incredible built-in defenses, it already is secure."

"That's a great idea, sir," Sean said. "Defending the White House would be a whole lot easier than defending your family compound. Besides that, it alleviates the problem of housing and food for the security force."

"We'd have to move Jones's wife and daughters back into the vacant vice presidents' mansion," the president continued, "and that's an insensitive thing to do during their period of mourning."

"Yeah, even though they're morning a scoundrel," Bobby said.

Sean offered, "Besides, Jones' family may not even want to stay in Washington. They may prefer to stay on their ranch. Look at what he has done to you, Mr. President with all due respect; I wouldn't be concerned with moving his wife and kids out of the White House. It's your residence. They violently took it from you. Do you think they gave one hoot about your family having to move? Don't be so hard on yourself, Mr. President. In my opinion, you and the kids would be much safer there."

"Speaking of kids, with all the confusion I didn't even ask if someone was looking after my family," the president said. "We'll need to let them know of our change in plans. Sean, I'll need you to send some people to make sure they're OK."

"Mr. President," the general said without hesitation, "I already thought of that. When Bobby called me with the Tiberius code and I knew you were about to go public, in an abundance of caution I had a twenty-four-hour guard put on your home in Georgetown. I didn't tell Mrs. Kelley because I didn't want them to worry about what was going on. They're safe Mr. President. Bobby, I did the same at your place in Virginia, and I even sent my security people to Kenny O'Donnell's home in Arlington Heights as well. Mr. President, in case you haven't noticed, if you'll look out your window and slightly to the rear, you'll see I also arranged to have two F-16s escort us on our trip north."

"Sean, you've thought of everything," Jack said appreciatively.

"These guys aren't going to get you on my watch, Mr. President," the general said.

"OK then, we're set. We are all in agreement: we're headed back to Washington and the White House. Bobby, let me borrow your cell while you and Sean continue to discuss this. I need to call Jackie."

"Jack, is that really you? I've missed you so much," Jackie said after hearing her husband's voice for the first time in nine months.

"Did you catch my address to the nation?" Jack asked.

"Of course I did, honey. I can't wait to see you and hug you. You have no idea what a nightmare these last months have been. To have been sitting next to you one minute and then seeing you whisked away the next minute fighting to stay alive, and then not hearing how you were doing for days on end, and not being able to see you, it's been terrible."

"Well it's all over, Jackie. We'll be together in the next few hours. These last few days all I kept thinking about was you and the kids, I've wanted to call you but everyone thought it would be too risky. How are the kids?" "They're just fine Jack, they ask for you just about every day. We have all missed you so much", Jackie said.

"Jackie, I know I can never change what has happened these last few months, but I promise our life will be much different than it was before. We are going to do things together much more often, quiet dinners together, more time with the kids, I promise. I love you, and these last few weeks I've realized just how much. I'm making arrangements to move back into the White House. Stay there and pack a few days worth of clothes for you and the kids. You can get the rest of your stuff later. There are security people outside. When the time is right, I'll have them bring you to the White House. I want to make sure all is OK before you and the kids come. I love you, honey. I'll see you soon."

"I love you too, Jack."

"Sean, would you instruct the pilot to get clearance for our arrival at Reagan airport. And can you get me Kenny O'Donnell on the phone?"

"Kenny, how are you"! "Mr. President is that you?" "Yah Kenny. "Jack, I can't tell you how good it is just to hear your voice," O'Donnell replied. "Kenny, I want you to go back to the White House," the president said to O'Donnell a few minutes later. "Arrange for Jones's wife and daughters to be moved back into the vice president's mansion."

"You have heard the news Jack haven't you," Kenny interrupted, "the President, I mean Jones, committed suicide. Actually, his wife and kids are in Texas on their ranch."

"Well, that eliminates one problem," Jack said. "Kenny, I want you to get with some of our Secret Service friends and have them sweep my limo to be sure its safe, and then send it to Regan National airport to pick up Bobby and me. Sean is arranging to have several military vehicles meet us at the airport to transport his men. Arrange for only two motorcycle police escorts, since we have plenty of security.

"And Kenny, we need to alert the White House security people that I will be arriving along with several dozen heavily armed soldiers. Make sure they know they need to stand down for now until we are safely back inside. Also Kenny, Jackie has a four-man security detail guarding her at my Georgetown home. Wait until I'm on the ground and on my way back to the White House before you send a limo to pick them up."

"Will do," O'Donnell said.

"And Kenny, thank you," the president continued. "I don't know how to adequately say how I feel. Thank you for being my friend. I can't imagine how difficult it must have been to go through all you've been through this past year. Thank you my friend!"

About thirty-five minutes later, with Air Force One about forty minutes out of Regan airport, Kenny made a call from the White House to Bobby's cell phone. He asked Bobby to put the president on the line.

"Mr. President," "yah Kenny," Jack replied, "I'm here at the White House and Jones's staff is in total confusion. Thank God most of them are gone for the weekend. The phones are ringing off the hook; people are calling from all over the world. There have been calls from Putin, Blair, Schroeder, Charac, Mobaric, and a number of others. I have instructed some of Jones's senior staff members, the few who are still here, to return calls to the heads of state advising them that you are in transit and will speak with them shortly. You must be exhausted Mr. President, but you'll need to get back to some of these people to calm them down."

"Kenny, listen to me, please stop Jones's people from making those calls. I'd like you to personally call each of them," President Kelley instructed. "They know how close you and I are. Tell them that all is well and that I'll be in touch with them in the next day or so. Coming from you, Kenny, it will mean so much more."

"I'll do it Mr. President," Kenny replied. By nine o'clock on Friday evening, the president had made his return to the White House. It had been a tumultuous day. The emergence of a President everyone thought was dead, the death of the sitting President under some very tragic circumstances, and the exposure of a far-reaching conspiracy to take over the United States.

Before going home for the night, Bobby arranged for a light dinner to be brought up for Jack and his family to share in the private residence upstairs. When they arrived at the White House, Jackie and the kids were immediately taken up upstairs. The president, advised they were there, waited for them to step off the elevator. As they reunited, Jack, Jackie, and the kids kissed and hugged each other in a four-way embrace that seemed to last forever. Jack felt exhausted as they walked toward the living room, but totally exhilarated at being reunited with his family. After spending a short time frolicking and playing with their father, the children comfortably settled into the bedrooms they had occupied before the Dallas ordeal. Jack and Jackie retired for the evening, leaving instructions not to be disturbed. They hadn't been together for nearly nine months.

Bobby and Kenny arrived at their homes at about 10 PM knowing they would have to be back early Saturday morning with full schedules for the whole weekend.

Thrilled by the day's events, their wives questioned them in great detail. For the first time, both were made aware of the dangers that had surrounded the president's recovery. Both were thankful that they had not been privy to every detail as it unfolded. Their wives had been careful during the past months not to ask too many questions, but now they wanted to know everything. They were amazed at the extensive evidence the Antonio group had uncovered. Having watched Jackie suffer for so long, both women were genuinely happy the first lady's ordeal was over, and they vowed to call her Saturday to let her know.

It was about 11 PM when Bobby called his assistant attorney general, a man by the name of Bill Dean. After about five minutes of conversation about the events of the day, Bobby told Dean that he wanted the special grand jury convened in an unusual Saturday morning session. Bill was a likable southern gentleman, a competent and tenacious attorney who had a long and successful career at the Justice Department. The day before the grand jury had issued over three-dozen subpoenas. Bobby wanted subpoenas issued on another two-dozen persons, the names of whom he rattled off to Dean. The list included some of the highest government officials in Washington. Bobby left it to Dean to prepare the necessary documents.

Bobby didn't even bother to include the names of those members of the Mafia he thought were involved. He fully expected he would learn the names of those individuals when he publicly questioned those involved on the fringes of the conspiracy. He could strike deals with these people to get more information about the individuals operating at the center of the conspiracy. He needed to build a pyramid of those involved from the bottom up. But Bobby Kelley's real intent was to have the names of these Mafia people revealed in public hearings. Once this happened, their own people might murder them. But either way the outcome suited him just fine. Kelley would either have his people do it or let the Mob insiders take care of them.

Arriving early Saturday morning at the White House, President Kelley's staff was back on duty, nearly to a person. They showed up spontaneously after learning of their former boss's miraculous survival. Thank God they all came—the telephone lines were jammed with calls from all over the world. Sean's security team had grown from twenty-four handpicked men to seventy-two, and everyone at the Pentagon now knew of his special mission to protect the president.

Soldiers were stationed at all locations where key members of President Kelley's staff worked. O'Donnell and Powers each had two armed security guards dressed in military garb stationed at their office. The White House resembled an armed camp under siege. As chief of staff, O'Donnell had called heads of state, scheduled the president to meet with leaders of the House and Senate, and done short interviews with the major television networks. Turning over the more distasteful tasks to his brother, the president handled the mending of political fences with Congress and foreign heads of state.

Bobby went to work Saturday morning with a four-man contingent of Sean's security team. He stationed two at the entrance to his office and two inside the office. Each member of the team was dressed in military garb and had automatic weapons at the ready. Arriving at his office, Bobby pulled out the chair at his desk and, as had happened the week before, saw a brown envelope sitting there. He had no idea who was sending him these envelopes. In all the commotion of this past week, he had totally neglected to view the security camera tapes Dan Lockman had brought to him that past Tuesday. Upon examining the contents of the envelope, he realized it was obvious that whoever had sent the letters was in the know about those inside the conspiracy. Evidently, the sender wanted to expose them. Bobby picked up the phone and dialed his administrative assistant.

"Shirley, I want you to call Dan Lockman," he instructed. "Ask him to get me the security-camera tapes from this wing of the building for the past thirty-six hours. Someone is leaving envelopes in my office, and I want to know how they're getting in here."

Shirley said, "I put that envelope on your chair, Mr. Kelley."

"What? Where did you get it, Shirley?"

"The mailroom delivered it to me yesterday afternoon. It had a note taped to it that said for Robert Kelley's eyes only."

Bobby had summoned to his office those individuals on his list of probable or possible conspirators who worked for the military or for the Secret Service team that had been part of the president's Dallas security detail. They also included members of the Werner Commission. Bobby asked each person to meet with him for an informal discussion. Anyone who refused would be served a subpoena by federal marshals. One of the first on the list was FBI Director Howard.

Two hours before the meetings, which didn't begin until 11 AM, Dean secretly convened the grand jury. For one and a half hours the assistant attorney general and a team of eight staff lawyers presented loose facts about the involvement of over two-dozen people in the conspiracy to assassinate the president. Caught up in the excitement of learning that the president survived the attempted assassination, the grand jury would all but rubber stamp whatever Assistant Attorney General Dean wanted. Over two-dozen more grand jury subpoenas were issued.

Director Howard entered Bobby's office full of praise and excitement that the president had survived. Bobby calmly asked Howard to have a seat and asked the FBI director if he would like a beverage. Howard declined, and the meeting began in earnest. Bobby's first question to Howard was, "Jay, I'm not going to beat around the bush. What did you know about the assassination before November 22?"

"I knew nothing about the assassination beforehand," the director stated forcefully.

"What do you know about the conspiracy surrounding the assassination?"

Again, the director's answer was adamant giving short but to the point answers. "I knew absolutely nothing about a conspiracy," he said.

Bobby then he asked him, "What do you know about a report marked top secret from the Rome, Italy, station chief Morgantheau?"

Knowing Morgantheau worked for the CIA, the director said, "The report you are referring to, Mr. Kelley, is a CIA report, and you know that I am not privy to such reports. I know nothing about it."

Bobby stood up and handed the director a subpoena to appear before the grand jury on Tuesday, three days from then. He said to Howard, "I told you I was not going to beat around the bush. I have absolute proof that you received a copy of the report and then just sat on it. If you're going to lie, you'll lie before the grand jury."

Continuing to plead ignorance, Howard shot back, "What's so important about this report anyway?"

Raising his voice a notch or two, Bobby informed the director, "You know as well as I do that that report lists the names of the men hired to shoot the president. It contains pictures, and it shows without doubt that both high-level Italian government officials and Mafia figures in Italy confirmed these were the men who attempted to kill my brother. And you and your CIA buddies sat on the report and did nothing. At the very least, that's obstruction of justice."

He motioned to the security people. "Get this son of a bitch out of my office. You're fired, you bastard."

"You can't fire me," Howard said. "I've been here a quarter century and have seen people like you come and go."

Ignoring Howard's remarks, Kelley continued, "If I find you back in this building, I'll have you arrested for trespassing. And before you go, let me leave you with one thought. You know those Mob people you've protected all these years, how do you think they are going to react when stories start appearing that you're going to tell everything you know about who was involved in the assassination?"

Kelley then ordered two security guards to accompany the director to his office, where he would be given five minutes to remove his personal effects before being escorted off the premises. This was the last attempt at friendly conversation that Kelley would attempt. Watching Howard walk out of his office, Bobby said, "I know everything, Jay, and I am going to make sure you swing slowly. I'm not only going to destroy your reputation, I am going to physically destroy you. Get out of my sight, you son of a bitch."

Next on Bobby's list of appointments was the Secret Service agent who had changed the direction of the president's motorcade in Dallas. The change, which was made at the last minute, caused the president's car to slow down and swing closer to the assassins' positions. Agent Phil Morrison was a seasoned Secret Service veteran who had served for over twenty years. His father, Steve, had grown up on Long Island with a number of streetwise low-level hoods. Steve was a gambler who ran numbers and took bets on horses. He had been convicted of trying to fix several horse races by bribing the jockeys, and had been barred from going to any para mutual racetrack.

Steve was determined that his son would not live the same kind of life he had. He struggled, but still managed to put Phil through NYU and then helped him get an MBA at Johnstown. But Phil was living a lie. He had been secretly having an affair with a woman for years, and he was his father's son when it came to gambling. Phil enjoyed going to Vegas and Reno and betting far more than he could afford to lose.

When Phil came into Bobby's office, he already seemed very nervous. Bobby's tactic was to pretend to know much more than he actually did.

"Phil, what have you been thinking about?" Bobby said, starting the conversation with a bang. "You're married twenty-five years and have four beautiful kids, but you've been seeing Gail Parker for years and you frequently go on gambling trips where you lose thousands of dollars."

"Do you think I'm going to sit here and let you verbally abuse me?" Morrison said.

"Now, I want you to understand something," Bobby continued. "With all my brother and I have been through, I am not going to play games with you. I am not going to allow you to double-talk me and claim you know nothing about the assassination. Do you see these guys behind you? They are sworn to serve my brother. They're Special Forces military. We have over 150 of them who will whack whoever we send them to whack. Do you understand where I'm coming from? I have enough information to legally indict you. By the way, here is your subpoena to appear before the grand jury next Thursday. Now, with that said, and knowing that I would really prefer revenge and would love to turn my back on how this information is extracted from you, I want you to tell me what you know about these bastards who tried to kill my brother. Start with telling me who told you to change the motorcade route.

"One more thing—before you begin, let me also tell you that if you lie to me about what you are about to say, I will not give you a second chance to tell me another lie. I will even up the score, just like they tried to do to my brother. Now that we completely understand each other, what can you tell me about the attempted assassination, Phil?"

Taken aback, Morrison hesitated for a moment and then told Bobby, "They'll kill me if I talk."

Leaning closer to Morrison, Bobby said, "So I guess you don't believe me when I tell you, so will I. But let me also say, I will make sure you suffer before you die. We'll break every bone in your body to get you to give up this scum you are protecting. If you don't begin to tell me something of substance within the next minute or so, I'll ask you to get up and leave. If I do that, God help you Phil, I'll turn this over to others, and I can assure you, they'll get you to talk. Read into this Phil. We are not playing games. One way or another, you're going to tell us what we want to know."

Relenting, Morrison began by saying "While I was in Reno back in February of last year, a guy in civilian dress who I later found out was a two-star general, a guy by the name of Bill Daley, approached me while I was playing craps. I had lost over $7,500 the week before, and was losing another $1,500 when we accidentally met at the craps table. Looking back, I guess it wasn't so accidental.

"Daley knew the croupier and suggested that he had inside connections. He said I couldn't lose and that I should place several bets alongside his. He was right. We both hit. Before I knew it, I was up $1,500 and we were having dinner together. I asked him if he was always that lucky. He said it isn't luck. He told me that he had done some favors for some people who wanted to show their appreciation. So they provided a first-class air ticket and comped a suite at Caesar's. When he started to gamble, he found that he had a credit of $10,000 to draw upon. Not only that, it seemed as though he couldn't lose. While I was with him, he won over twenty grand. Tagging along on his bets, I won five grand for myself."

"Go on, Phil," Bobby instructed.

"So I asked Daley, 'What kind of favors do you have to do to warrant this kind of appreciation? More importantly, who in the world has the kind of power to arrange for someone to win at the craps table? That takes some doing.'

"'Nah,' said Daley, 'from what I understand, these guys frequently send politicians, judges, you name it here to collect for favors. It's relatively clean. This is my fifth time in three years. Last time I won $23,000, but I've won as much as $45,000 in a year. You come here, stay in a nice room, have some good food, and when you walk up to the tables, they make sure you win. Even people standing next to you don't know what's going on. I don't know how they do it, but they do. You even pay taxes on what you win before you leave. What a great system.'

"'You asked what I did to deserve this,' General Daley said to me. 'Well, I'm a two-star Army general. Every year a certain amount of government inventory becomes obsolete. I'm in charge of getting rid of it. Sometimes the government gets rid of some perfectly good stuff. I just make sure certain people have the winning bid when they want something. They get a list of what the government and the military have coming up for auction, and they call me to express an interest in a certain lot number. The only thing anyone could ever accuse me of is being lucky at the craps table.'"

Morrison shrugged. "I figured it must have been some really connected people who could arrange that."

As Morrison continued to tell Kelley his story, he said, "A few months after the February encounter with the general in Reno, I learned in a conversation with my father that some of the people the general mentioned he was doing favors for were the bosses of some of the Mob guys my dad knew. After that, I couldn't believe that bumping into this general was just a coincidence.

"When they finally made their move and approached me, I was all ready for the trip to Dallas with President Kelley. I was told I'd be part of the president's advance security team, as I had been on a number of other occasions. The first day I was there, the hotel desk clerk gave the other three agents and me a complimentary voucher for dinner and drinks at a local restaurant and bar. Actually, it was a strip joint, but it had great food. We all took them up on the offer. The dinner was great and we couldn't put our hands in our pockets. They must have bought the four of us three or four drinks each." Morrison continued with his story.

"As we were leaving, our waiter pulled me aside and asked me if I knew General Daley. I couldn't believe that he just happened to be our waiter and also just happened to know Bill Daley. Instead of answering, I asked him what it was that he wanted. This waiter simply said he would arrange for me to win $50,000 in Vegas. All I had to do was redirect the lead car in the president's motorcade to take a left just a few feet past where it was planned for him to turn. Look at it you'll see where I mean. Do it and I'll be in touch within 3 or 4 weeks to arrange your trip."

"I left there thinking I needed to report this incident, but then I thought I would have to expose Daley, and I was nervous about where that might lead. Some of the people the general knew also knew my dad. I thought that if that became public knowledge, it might cost me my job. So when I got back to the hotel, I pulled out the map of the route the motorcade would take. Frankly, I didn't think it was a big deal to take that second left. After all, it was only about fifteen or twenty-five feet out of the way. I thought they were putting me through some sort of test and were doing it to hook me so they could have me do something bigger in the future. I really didn't think it was a big deal, and I really needed the money to cover my gambling debts. In fact I now believe that just as they arranged for certain people to win at the tables, they had me losing to put pressure on me." Morrison continued.

"I changed the left turn because I didn't see anything wrong with doing it. It wasn't until after the president was shot that I realized that the waiter was involved in the assassination, and that he used me to make sure the president's limo would have to slow down to navigate a much sharper left. I swear I didn't understand the significance of what I was doing. After that, I was terrified to come forward. And then they killed that poor guy they claimed shot the president. I realized that the guy who killed Osborn was the owner of the restaurant we'd eaten at that night before the assassination. I was convinced they would kill me if I came forward.

"Mr. Kelley, I didn't know that what I was doing would result in such a terrible outcome. Here we are nearly ten months later, and no one ever even asked me why I changed the turn. I was expecting to be called before the Werner Commission, but I guess they just didn't want to hear from me."

Bobby stood up and walked around his desk. He paused for a moment and then said, "Will you step outside and work with one of our criminal artists to create a sketch of the waiter and desk clerk? I'll decide what I'm going to do with you later. In the meantime, I want you to report to me immediately if any of these people contact you for any reason. Did anyone ever call you to set up the trip to Vegas they promised?" Morrison shook his head indicating no one had contacted him.

Bobby walked over to his closed office door and beckoned for his secretary, "Shirley set Mr. Morrison up with an artist and be sure I get a copy of the renditions." As Morrison began to leave with Bobby's secretary, Bobby said, "Mr. Morrison I will be calling you in a few days for further questioning".

Next on Bobby's list of visitors was the chief counsel to the Werner Commission, a man by the name of Arlund Spacer. Spacer had previously served on several congressional investigations and was well connected with members of Congress on both sides of the aisle. It was Spacer who first introduced the idea that one bullet hit the president, passed through his body, then hit the governor in the shoulder, exited the governor's shoulder, hit him in the wrist and then entered his leg. This same bullet was found lying on a stretcher at the hospital.

With all the damage it did, hitting bone in several areas of the governor's body, this bullet was found on a stretcher at the hospital with hardly a mark on it.

As Spacer entered Kelley's office the men shook hands. Once Spacer had taken a seat, Bobby said, "So Mr. Spacer, I've been following your activities these past several months. You've been all over the TV and newspapers. With all this publicity, you should run for office. Tell me, how did you come up with the idea that one bullet did all that damage? Do you have any background in such things?"

"Actually Mr. Kelley, I have worked with ballistics people for quite a few years, dating back to my days as a prosecutor. It might surprise you to know that I have more than a respectable knowledge of ballistics."

Bobby could not pass up a chance to go after Spacer's cockiness. "I suppose that's why you were chosen to put forth such a ridiculous supposition. You honestly believe that one bullet hit my brother's head and then shattered the governor's shoulder, wrist, and knee without any appreciable signs of damage to the bullet?"

"Mr. Kelley, I have several experienced ballistics experts that say that's exactly what happened."

"That's a lie, Mr. Spacer, and you know it. Your own ballistics experts' report, a copy of which I have right here, shows there was no trace of blood on that bullet. All of their tests show the bullet could not have survived after hitting all that bone without sustaining substantial damage. Yet the bullet you claim was the one used in the assassination was nearly pristine. You may be able to pass that flawed theory off with your cronies on the Werner Commission, but do you think the rest of us are that stupid? The Werner Commission was deliberately vague about such matters and flat out refused to publicly release the names of those experts. But maybe you would be kind enough to provide me with a list of those ballistics experts."

"Certainly," Spacer replied, "but I'll need to get permission from the majority of the commission members before I can provide you with that information."

"Mr. Spacer, I don't think you understand. I am, as the chief law enforcement officer of the United States, conducting an investigation into the conspiracy surrounding the attempted assassination of the president of the United States. You can either cooperate, or I'll have you thrown in jail as a coconspirator. I can assure you it will take months for you to prove that you are not a threat to our country's national security.

"And since you have just set the tone for your cooperation or lack thereof, let me officially provide you with your subpoena to appear before the grand jury investigating the assassination. Let me also tell you that a lot of people are going to be put in jail for their part in this conspiracy. You can decide to play ball with us and tell us all you know, or you can be treated like the enemy."

"Mr. Kelley," Spacer replied, "I was hired by the chief justice to be lead counsel to his commission. I did a good job. I was conscientious and did nothing wrong. Of course I'll appear before your grand jury, and you can investigate all you want, but you'll find I did nothing wrong. We called 552 witnesses and received ten federal agency reports, from the FBI, CIA, DIA, Secret Service, and State Department. Our final report submitted to President Jones contained twenty-six volumes."

As Spacer stood to leave, Bobby told him, "I'm sure you covered your ass well, Mr. Spacer. I'm also aware that the Werner Commission knew even before they called their first witness that they would conclude that a lone assassin killed my brother and that he did so without the help of anyone else. I will prove that they decided that would be their finding even before they convened their first meeting.

"We are both also aware that dozens of eyewitnesses offered to testify on matters which could have proved other people were involved, and that you personally decided they would not be called before the commission. These extremely credible eyewitness accounts of the assassination were not pursued because this testimony would have been in direct conflict with the commission's predetermined findings."

In an effort to convince Spacer to turn state's evidence, Robert Kelley continued his verbal assault. "We are also both aware that the testimony given by many witnesses that you did call, Mr. Spacer, pointed to substantial evidence that others were involved. You and the committee chose to ignore much of that evidence. Why, you guys didn't even allow for an attorney to act on behalf of Osborn during cross-examinations of your so-called witnesses until weeks into the investigation. And even after one was appointed, he wasn't allowed to attend any of your top-secret hearings. This so-called advocate for the rights of Osborn never cross-examined a single witness. What kind of Supreme Court chief justice would trample on the constitutional rights of a U.S. citizen and conduct secret hearings into the assassination of the president? That's what you were a party to. Is that what you call doing nothing wrong?"

"Mr. Spacer, I don't know if I can prove you had anything to do with the attack on the president, but knowingly or unknowingly, acting either out of fear or complicity with those involved in the assassination, you sure as hell were involved in its cover-up."

Spacer had had enough of Kelley's verbal abuse. He stormed out of Kelley's office without saying a word. But Bobby had a feeling in the pit of his stomach that Spacer would be in touch with him soon, and of his own free will.

"Shirley, I'm on my way over to the White House, why don't you go home to your family, I'll see you Monday morning. Bobby went by O'Donnell's office to ask about his brother's schedule. He was concerned about Jack's health. The man had been thrust into a crazy schedule before he'd had enough time to convalesce, and Bobby didn't want him to have a relapse. Only eight days earlier he'd been in a hospital. He needed more time to build his strength.

Worried that Jack was overdoing, Bobby told O'Donnell, "You're going to have to find ways to build some rest time into his schedule. It might be a good idea if you and Jackie schedule him for a two-hour lunch each day for the next few weeks. And Kenny, don't let him get talked into any travel. He has the election coming up, and he's going to want to be out there stomping for reelection. The American people are going to reelect Jack by a landslide, so no travel or at least very little, and under extremely tight conditions, OK?"

Bobby asked O'Donnell if had seen Sean. O'Donnell told him that Sean had set up office in the West Wing of the White House. He would organize and operate his security forces there until he felt secure in reestablishing security ties with the Secret Service. Having come down from the residence Saturday morning to a White House that appeared to be under siege, President Kelley requested that Sean's men wear business suits and conceal their automatic weapons.

CHAPTER 12

▼

GETTING EVEN, NOT MAD

Bobby Kelley walked into Sean's office, closing the door behind him and taking a seat he tossed the brown envelope he had received from the mysterious insider onto Sean's desk, then explained how he had received it.

"This is explosive stuff, Bobby. What do you think we should do with it?" Sean asked. The envelope contained the Morgantheau report, six typewritten pages on the three shooters, and a mug shot of each. The shooters' names were Mario Friscatti, Anthony Caprielli, and Salvatore Falcone. The report was dated December 5, 2003, just two weeks after the assassination. The report listed the names of their stateside connections, and all were known associates of the New York/New Jersey mafia. Each shooter had received three hundred thousand dollars worth of heroin at dealer value, which they could sell on the street for $1–1.5 million. All three were Corsicans, and all three were professional contract killers belonging to a Mafia coalition of over twenty members who had vowed revenge should one of them be double-crossed.

"These guys will never talk, Sean. They were chosen because they have a reputation for obeying their code of silence. They'll never help us identify anyone else who was involved. Besides, they probably don't even know who else was involved. They are contract killers, and they need to die. Can you arrange that, Sean?"

"It will take some time and planning but yes, I can," Sean replied.

"I want to send these bastards a loud and clear message," Bobby said. "It will scare the shit out of some of them here in the States, and that should fit well with the upcoming investigation I'm planning. Maybe I can shake a few of these bastards into telling me everything they know. Hopefully I'll be able to get a few names out of them. I'm going to get to the bottom of this and expose every last one of these bastards. Who knows, maybe we can get a few more of them to commit suicide."

"I'll let you know before I put things into motion, Bobby," Sean said.

"No, Sean," Bobby cautioned. "I don't want to know anything about it. Do whatever you need to do, but for God's sake, be careful. These guys came damn close to killing my brother and succeeded in actually taking over the United States for nine months, so be very deliberate and very, very careful. I don't want one of our guys to get hurt. There's no need for hand-to-hand combat. Do it from a distance if you can. And Sean, the fewer people who are involved in this, the better. These creeps don't deserve to continue to live, much less live the life of Riley."

With that Bobby stood up and started toward the door. "Monday will be here before we know it. I think I'm going home to spend some time with my wife and kids. Why don't you get out of here, Sean? It's been a crazy week for all of us."

In the weeks that followed his return to the White House, President Kelley attended to matters of state and to mending relations with heads of state, many of whom were badly shaken by the uncertainty of the events surrounding the assassination attempt and the suicide of President Jones. Robert Kelley, on the other hand, was single-minded. He spent his days trying to fulfill his mission to expose every last person who had anything to do with his brother's attempted murder.

Numerous personal accounts of the assassination were leaked to Bobby and his investigators. Some of the leaks were in the form of copies of internal memos sent anonymously to Kelley's investigators. The language used in these memos was veiled and sometimes confusing, unless viewed alongside the many similar documents. Only then did the messages make any sense, and only then did the shape of the conspiracy begin to take shape exposing its' participants.

These professional investigators were a group made up of lawyers and military and political strategists. They cataloged thousands of bits of information and slowly pieced together what had happened in the days before and after the attempted assassination. Thousands of hours were spent piecing together minute details about individuals they suspected of being involved. Here is some of what they recorded.

The first shot was fired at the president at 12:31 PM. Eyewitness accounts of dozens of spectators suggest that the actions of the police, CIA, Secret Service, FBI, and local officials were somewhat chaotic at first glance.

But upon closer examination Kelley and his investigators realized that what had happened was anything but chaotic. Rather, they were a well-orchestrated series of maneuvers which started to unfold almost immediately after President Kelley's limo went speeding away to the hospital with its wounded occupant.

Moments after the shots were fired, over a dozen Secret Service agents and CIA agents began working their way through the crowd of people lined up along the president's motorcade route. The agents confiscated film from the cameras of ordinary citizens. Dozens of people testified that they were shown official Secret Service and CIA badges and ordered to hand over their film. Such actions had to have been planned in advance; such a reaction, with so many agents involved, could not have happened spontaneously. None of the documentation on the investigation, including the Werner Commission documentation, made mention of where any of the film could be found or who the agents had turned the film over to. The Kelley team's conclusion was that the agents had preexisting knowledge of the assassination and that those involved in the agencies had destroyed the film so it would never be made publicly available.

A particularly noteworthy Polaroid photo was confiscated from a woman named Maryanne Wearman who had been standing across from the grassy knoll. Wearman had snapped a photo of the president passing in front of her within one-sixteenth of a second after the first shot hit the president. She was so shaken by having her film confiscated that she never again used that camera. She was later approached by two university professors who wanted to use computer enhancement methods to see if they could develop an image of the photo, which was burned onto the camera's paper packing. Ms. Wearman agreed to allow the professors to experiment with the camera.

Polaroid film is loaded into a camera containing light-sensitive paper, which protects the actual film from premature exposure. It was this light-sensitive paper which, once computer enhanced, shows one of the assassins in what appears to be a police uniform. The assassin is holding a rifle to his face, and the muzzle of the gun has smoke coming from it. The gun was pointed at the president, and the photo was snapped at the split second the gun was fired. The investigators named the assassin in the photo the "badge man." This was the same gunman that dozens of very credible witnesses came forward to testify about. The Werner Commission ignored this solid eyewitness evidence that more than one gunman was involved in shooting the president.

Mrs. Wearman was interviewed by a number of news organizations. She stated that she was absolutely certain of what she saw on November 22. There was no question in her mind that she saw the shot fired from behind the fence on the grassy knoll. She watched in horror as she saw the president's head explode, with human tissue blown to the rear and left of him. The impact of the shot threw his body back and to the rear left, towards Mrs. Kelley. Mrs. Wearman said, "No one can persuade me differently, and I will go to my grave convinced of what I saw that day." She was never asked to testify before the Werner Commission, despite her celebrated interviews by several TV stations. Her testimony would have totally contradicted the prearranged findings of the Werner Commission, so they simply ignored her.

The Antonio group also learned that standing on the grassy knoll across the street from Mrs. Wearman was a man named Jacob Zepuder who had come to watch the presidential motorcade. Zepuder had an 8 mm movie camera and filmed the president as the motorcade drove by. He captured the entire assassination on film. Immediately after the president's limo sped away, realizing what he had filmed, he went to the United Press International (UPI) Dallas bureau to have his film developed.

When the UPI Dallas bureau manager developed the film and realized what Zepuder had captured, he got on his direct line to UPI's New York office and spoke with Franklin Coffey, the New York bureau photo editor. It was Coffey's job to determine which photos would move, and on what portion of the network.

Zepuder wanted five hundred thousand dollars for his film. UPI vice president Frank Tremain, a renowned former war photo correspondent himself, had to get permission from his superiors to pay such a large sum of money. The negotiation between Zepuder and Tremain went back and forth. Handing the phone to Coffey, Tremain left to get the go-ahead to pay Zepuder the outrageous sum of money he was demanding. with the instructions, "don't let him get off that phone until I get back." So Coffey spoke to Zepuder and asked him to describe what had happened. He figured as long as Zepuder stayed on the phone, Tremain wouldn't be angry.

Talking with Zepuder, Coffey learned how certain Zepuder was that the bullets had come from immediately behind him. Zepuder said that he had been standing just twenty or so feet from the fence that faced the president's car, and that he had seen the president being hit by the bullets. His film told the story better than thousands of words could have. There it was, for all to see. Ultimately the Zepuder film was shared between *Life* magazine and UPI. The government later confiscated it.

The Zepuder film and the images from Mrs. Wearman's camera, which were computer enhanced, fit perfectly together. They gave a photo report of what might have been the last seconds of the president's life. Mrs. Wearman had faced the president from his left side. Her Polaroid photo showed what happened from that perspective. It captured the outline of the assassin with the gun to his shoulder aiming at the president at the exact moment he fired the *right front headshot*. The part of the Zepuder film that corresponded to this precise time showed the president's right side and the impact of the bullets as they hit the president. None of this ever made it to the Werner Commission, as they did not consider it "credible evidence."

Shortly after the Dallas bureau sent the first Zepuder photos over the UPI network, the FBI confiscated the entire film. They even sent FBI agents to the New York UPI bureau to confiscate wastepaper baskets to make sure none of the transmitted photos, or even parts of them, survived. Despite their attempts to limit the photos media exposure, a number of these photos made it into publication, Zepuder sued the government. Using every legal ploy available, the Jones administration tied up the release of the film for as long as it could. Although the federal government continued to claim the film was confiscated for national security reasons, the Federal Appeals Court eventually awarded the Zepuder family $8 million to compensate them for what they had lost.

There were several dozen ordinary people standing on the grassy knoll that day watching the president's motorcade pass by. Every picture of that event showed that they all hit the ground at the sound of the shots, many looking behind them at the fence on top of that knoll. A Dallas police officer who saw the shots fired from behind the fence left the street and started up the hill on his motorcycle. At least eighteen people who had stood on the railroad bridge also came forward and volunteered that they had seen a man fire a rifle from behind the wooded fence on top of the knoll. None were ever questioned by the Werner Commission,

The bullet found by a CIA agent on a stretcher used to carry the governor into the hospital was later tested and found to have been shot from the same rifle the government claimed was used by the lone assassin. The bullet was nearly pristine, with almost no damage to it. Ballistics experts determined it would be impossible for a bullet to be in such pristine condition after going through bone and tissue and then emerge without a trace of damage and no bone, blood, or tissue embedded in it. Yet it had rifle markings that showed it was shot from the rifle the government claimed the assassin used. If any reasonable man examined the facts of the bullet alone, the Antonio group concluded, he would almost certainly determine that the bullet had been fired from that rifle beforehand and then placed on the stretcher at the hospital by someone who was part of the conspiracy.

In addition, on the day of the assassination the government produced a rifle they claimed was ordered by the lone assassin (Osborn) via mail order. The rifle was completely wiped clean and had absolutely no fingerprints on it. Yet a copy of the Osborn order provided by the mail-order company showed the rifle they had sent Osborn was a different make and caliber than the one the government had produced.

The Antonio group investigators summarized some of their findings in a report to the senior members of the group. A pristine bullet was found lying on a stretcher at the hospital emergency room. Ballistics tests showed the bullet had been fired from the rifle the Dallas police force said was Osborn's, but the bullet had no damage to it and contained no blood, tissue, or bone residue. In addition, mail-order company records showed that a rifle purchased by Osborn was of a different make and caliber than the rifle the Dallas police force produced as being Osborn's.

A very credible newsman who was at the hospital when the wounded president was brought in reported that he had had a conversation with Jack Sarubi in front of the Parkland Hospital emergency room. Why would Jack Sarubi have been at that hospital at the very moment the wounded president arrived? Several months after the shooting, the newsman reported to the Antonio group that he had thought nothing of seeing Sarubi at the hospital until two days later, when Sarubi shot and killed the so-called lone assassin. The investigators were baffled by Sarubi's actions. Why would Sarubi have done what he did knowing there was no chance of escape? In a two-day period Sarubi's actions totally altered his life. On Thursday he entertained the President's Secret Service detail the night before the assassination, buying them dinner and drinks' keeping them out until the wee hours of the morning less than 8 hours before the President was to arrive? On Friday a friend of 20 years reported talking with him at the Parkland hospital as Kelley arrived.

On Sunday he is standing four feet from Osborn as he is lead out of the police station, and fatally shoots him. Investigators concluded that there were parts of their inquiry that could never be brought full circle—there were individual motives at play that had little or nothing to do with why the assassination took place.

The investigators did, however, have hard evidence that refuted the very premise of the official findings. This evidence indicated that, consistent with a shot fired from the president's right front side, several motorcycle police officers traveling behind the president's limo were spattered with blood, hair, and skull and tissue fragments. Zepuder's pictures showed these motorcycle officers were some ten feet behind the limo. Had the fatal shot come from behind and above the president, as the Werner Commission claimed in its report, the tissue matter would have traveled forward, to the front of the president.

CHAPTER 13

▼

ASSASSIN OR PATSY?

Leonard Osborn, the man the Werner Commission claimed shot President Kelley, had a complex background. Given the facts—according to the CIA, he was a communist sympathizer—most Americans would have despised the man. But he was well chosen by the conspirators. The absolute genius of their plan was that they convinced Osborn he was involved but never let him in on what was really going on. At the moment the true assassins fired their weapons, Osborn was sitting with a manager on the second floor of the book depository. Everyone who testified agreed that the Dallas police arrived at the sixth-floor window they claimed the shots were fired from within ninety seconds of the attack.

On their way up to the sixth floor of the book depository, several Dallas police officers passed the second-floor luncheon area where, both police officers and the manager testified, Osborn was seated with a manager having coffee. The manager testified that Osborn had been there with him at least several minutes before the police arrived. He was not out of breath or winded, but rather was calmly having a conversation with the manager. When he saw the police officers running by, he asked what the commotion was all about. One of the police officers told him that the president had been shot, from the sixth floor of the depository. Osborn may have been stupid, but he was not that stupid. He realized immediately that he had been set up as a patsy. He had been reporting to the CIA about a terrorist group's plans to kill the president, when all along the "terrorists" were actually CIA. Once Osborn realized he had been set up, he quietly left the building and got on a city bus to go home. Although several people testified that they saw Osborn on the second floor of the depository less than ninety seconds after the shooting, the government insisted he was a lone assassin firing from the sixth floor.

The Werner Commission claimed that Osborn fired three incredibly accurate shots that hit the president in the head and throat in eight seconds. They claimed he then dropped the rifle and ran across the width of the warehouse, down four flights of stairs, and was sitting having coffee with a manager on the second floor when the police rushed in. The manager made a statement to the police that Osborn was with him for several minutes, and several eyewitnesses claimed he was not winded or out of breath. None of the women who were walking down the stairs at the moment the president was shot could remember seeing Osborn in the staircase. And could anyone seriously believe that Osborn's getaway plan was to shoot the President of the United States and then use public transportation as his get away?

Within hours of Osborn's arrest, the government released a photo of him holding what they claimed was the rifle used in the assassination. When asked by a reporter about the photo, Osborn claimed, "That's not me in that picture. They must have doctored it." Anyone looking closely at the photo, which was taken outdoors on a sunny day, would have noticed that Osborn's body was casting a shadow to the right just behind him, as would happen if it were about 2:30 PM. But another shadow, cast onto Osborn's face by his nose, indicated that the sun was overhead, as if the picture had been taken at 12 noon. The photo had clearly been doctored. If the government didn't doctor the photo why would they release a photo they knew or should have known was doctored by someone?

The government's case against Osborn would never have survived a trial. In fact, there was so little evidence against him that he may never have been indicted. If the case had gone to trial, prosecutors would have faced an uphill battle.

Because of the lengthily interrogation of Osborn conducted by police and federal agents without his attorney present, the case against Osborn would have faced an up hill battle; his defense lawyer would have been constantly petitioning the court to disallow much of what prosecutors would have attempted to introduce as evidence. The Antonio investigators concluded that insiders at the FBI, CIA, and Dallas police force must have known the case would never make it to the courtroom. Without police "cooperation," there would have been no way for a man with Jack Sarubi's background to wind up standing four feet from Osborn with a pistol in his hand.

The conspirators did pick the perfect fall guy, however. Born on October 18, 1977 in New Orleans, Leonard Osborn moved with his family a number of times during his childhood. By the time he enlisted in the U.S. Marine Corps for basic training, he had moved twenty times in seventeen years, from New Orleans to Dallas to Covington, Louisiana, to Fort Worth, Texas, to New York to the Bronx, back to New Orleans and then back to Fort Worth. With each move Osborn found it harder to develop any meaningful relationships. He was unable to put down roots, and moving in and out of different schools made schoolwork even more difficult.

After having served four years in the Marines he was released from active duty, he sailed for Europe nine days later. He took a plane from London to Helsinki, and then to Moscow. After arriving in Moscow, acting either on instruction or simply because he was a confused, troubled person, he went to the U.S. Embassy and attempted to renounce his U.S. citizenship. During his stay in Russia, which lasted two years and seven months, he received 650 rubles every month from an unknown source. In letters to his brother he claimed to have no money problems at all. A question arises, how does a man living on the salary of a Marine travel by ship and plane to Russia, arrive in a strange country and 3 weeks later write that he has no financial worries at all? While in Russia he also married a Russian woman, Marina Brusakova.

Believing he was a CIA operative, the KGB kept Osborn under close surveillance throughout his stay in Russia. There is substantial circumstantial evidence that Osborn was in fact a CIA operative, even that far back. Before he entered the Marines, Osborn knew little or nothing about Russia or the Russian language. When he was discharged, however, he could speak fluent Russian and was more than simply familiar with Russian history. He spoke such fluent Russian his wife mistook him for a native the first time they met.

Upon returning to the United States from Russia, Osborn became active in a New Orleans group supporting communism in Cuba. It would be hard for anyone to downplay the fact that the offices used by the pro-Cuba group adjoined the offices used by the FBI, and that the CIA rented offices immediately across the street. In fact, the activist group used FBI printing equipment to produce the flyers it handed out at pro-Cuba rallies.

Osborn was arrested a little less than three hours after President Kelley was shot. He was questioned for hours by members of the Dallas police force, in the presence of Police Chief Jesse Curry, District Attorney Wade, and agents from the FBI, CIA, and the Secret Service. At one point while he was being moved within the police station, a reporter asked him where the bruises on his face had come from. Osborn replied, "The police beat me up."

When Robert Kelley learned that Dallas police had offered no protection to Osborn's wife and mother, despite numerous death threats being made against them, he was furious. He was even more appalled when he learned that these women, prior to giving their Werner Commission testimony, were separated and held in custody for nine weeks of questioning. The whole thing pointed to an attempt to brain wash the women.

All the commission meetings were held in secret, and all the information and evidence they received was classified as top secret. Why would evidence gathered by such a prominent group of government officials be classified top secret, especially if the alleged perpetrator acted alone? Didn't the people have a right to know?

Notes written by Werner Commission investigators claimed that the newspaper reporter who testified that Sarubi was at the hospital when the president was brought into the emergency room was mistaken. The reporter claimed he had a brief conversation with Sarubi at the hospital that day, the reporter had known Sarubi for over 20 years. It is not likely he could have been mistaken. Include the discovery of the pristine bullet, a bullet that had rifle markings from the gun they claimed was Osborn's—how could this be a coincidence? Investigators for the Kelleys concluded that this was just one more instance of the Werner Commission ignoring hard evidence that went against their intended findings.

When members of the Werner Commission later went to Dallas to interview Sarubi, he begged them to put him into protective custody. He promised that if they got him out of Dallas and away from the Dallas police, he would tell them everything he knew about the assassination. The commission members left Dallas, never making mention of Sarubi's offer to tell all. Very few people were permitted to visit Sarubi after he murdered Osborn, but everyone who did visit reported that Sarubi told them he was being injected with cancerous cells. The Antonio investigators thought this claim of Sarubi's was preposterous, at least until they began looking into it.

One of the people allowed to visit Sarubi in his Dallas jail cell was a TV reporter named Dorothy Kilherman. After a lengthy visit with Sarubi, Kilherman publicly announced, "I am assembling my notes, and will shortly break open the president's assassination case."

Just a few weeks after this announcement, she was found dead of an overdose of prescription drugs and alcohol. Her interview with Sarubi was never published. Two days after Kilherman died, her close friend and secretary, the woman

Kilherman entrusted with her notes on the case, also died, also of unnatural causes. A short time later Sarubi was diagnosed with cancer; he died within sixty days, never having had the chance to tell his side of the assassination story.

During their investigation, the Antonio group learned that Osborn had been having an affair with a nurse while he lived in New Orleans. The nurse assisted a university professor in his government-sponsored and funded research on cancer. The purpose of this research was not to find a cure for cancer, but to develop more lethal, faster acting strains of cancer that could be used as weapons. The investigators realized that Sarubi's claims were not as preposterous as they had first thought.

In all, there were over two hundred suspicious deaths of people who were in some way associated with the assassination. Some were people who were simply in the wrong place at the wrong time and witnessed something they should not have seen. Some were people who just by chance or circumstance had come to know too much. One such person, a railroad worker, viewed the "badge man" with his rifle on the grassy knoll. He told police he had also seen a man dressed in a police uniform put a rifle in a railroad switching box and walk off down the train tracks. He even described the man in detail. Hours later when police checked the switching box, the rifle was gone.

The Kelley investigation sorted through thousands of clues about the assassination. Some of the more disturbing involved how dozens of people who came forward with information were "eliminated." Among them were:

• Karin Capacineti, who was murdered ten months before the assassination. Capacineti was overheard talking about Jack Kelley's death before it was to have happened.

• Jack Zingaro, who died of a gunshot wound weeks after 11/22. Zingaro claimed to have known beforehand that Sarubi would shoot Osborn.

• Eddy Bernards, who died of a gunshot wound two months after 11/22. Bernards was the look-alike brother of Warren Bernards, who told others he had seen Officer Tibbit shooting death from his kitchen window.

• Betty Macaby, who "committed suicide" two months after 11/22. Macaby worked for Sarubi, and she gave an alibi for Warren Bernards the Tibbit shooting suspect.

- Bill Hester, who died of a "heart attack" three months after 11/22. Hester told others he had information linking Osborn to Jack Sarubi.

- Hank Hill, who had his throat cut and died three months after 11/22. Hill was the husband of a Sarubi employee, and knew many Osborn acquaintances.

- Bill Oster, who died from "accidental" causes four months after 11/22. Oster had visited Jack Sarubi's apartment the Sunday morning Sarubi killed Osborn.

- Gary Underwood, who died of a purportedly self-inflicted gunshot wound four months after 11/22. Underwood was a CIA agent, and claimed the agency was involved in the assassination.

- Hugh Parters, who was killed in a plane crash four months after 11/22. Parters was a private investigator who worked with FBI agents Guy Banister and David Ferrie.

- Billy Morris, who was killed in a plane crash six months after 11/22. Morris was the mayor of New Orleans, and he knew Banister, Marcello, and Tom Kaminski, Sarubi's lawyer.

- Guy Howard, who was dead from a "heart attack" six months after 11/22. Howard was an ex-FBI agent, connected to Ferrie, the CIA, Marcello, and Osborn.

- Jim Kather, who died of a blow to the head nine months after 11/22. Kather was in Jack Sarubi's apartment the Sunday Sarubi killed Osborn.

- Mary Parchman, who was murdered ten months after 11/22, and who was a "special" friend of Jack Kelley. Parchman's personal diary was confiscated by CIA chief James Angleton after her murder.

- Tom Kaminski, who died from an apparent heart attack fifteen months after 11/22. Kaminski was Sarubi's first lawyer, and was in Sarubi's apartment the day Osborn was killed.

- Rose Ceramison, who was killed in a hit and run twenty-two months after 11/22. Ceramison told many people that she had known about the assassination in advance.

- Dorothy Kilherman, drug overdose, died 2 years after 11/22 after a private interview with Sarubi, national columnist and TV person she claimed she would "break open" the assassination conspiracy.

- Mrs. Pat Smyth, cause of death unknown, died 2 days after Kilherman, she was Kilherman's secretary who kept her notes, they were never found.

- Karen Karlino, who died of a gunshot wound two years after 11/22. Karlino was the last person to speak with Sarubi before he killed Osborn.

- Capt. James Marlin, who died suddenly thirty months after 11/22. Marlin was a police officer who witnessed the Osborn slaying and later told the Werner Commission, "There's a lot to be said, but it would probably be better if I don't say it."

- Marilyn Smalle, who died of a gunshot wound thirty-two months after 11/22. Smalle was a dancer at Jack Sarubi's club.

- Lt. William Palsetti, who died of a gunshot wound thirty-five months after 11/22. Palsetti was the president's autopsy photographer. He described his duty as "a horrifying experience."

- Jack Sarubi, lung cancer, his claim, he was being injected with it.

- Dr. Mary Singleton, who died of a gunshot wound. Singleton led research into the use of cancer as a strategic weapon. Her assistant dated Osborn.

- Haley Biggs, who disappeared. Biggs was House majority leader and a member of the Werner Commission. Before he disappeared, he began to publicly express doubts about the Werner Commission's final report.

These are only some of the mysterious deaths that surrounded the assassination; many more could have been listed. Typical of the methods used for silencing those who oppose them, the Mob has developed ways of silencing people that attracts little if any attention. No longer is it necessary to execute someone in the same method used in the 1930's or 1950's. Science has not only developed for much of the civilized world, it has also developed for the uncivilized world as well.

Given the evidence, it is indisputable that the CIA was working closely with the Mafia. What could President Jones have been thinking when he appointed

Dunlap, fired by President Kelley from his position as CIA director just 16 months prior to the assassination attempt, to be a member of the Werner Commission investigating the assassination? It was like putting the fox in charge of the chicken coop. Director Dunlap had a reputation for being a master of deception and misinformation. He would ensure that the facts surrounding the assassination would never become public. Why would the Werner Commission hold all of its hearings behind closed doors? Why would all witness testimony be classified as top secret? Surely these events orchestrated by the chief justice and the former CIA director played well for those associated with the assassination attempt. Examining their individual motives played upon things that could never have been associated with the assassination and there in laid the genius of the intelligence surrounding the assassination attempt.

The former CIA director was asked by the chief justice, who was the chairman of the commission, to provide security for all commission members so they could investigate the assassination without feeling insecure about their physical safety. But what kind of message would that send to the commission members? When the evidence started coming in, the commission members would realize that the very people who were protecting them were the ones the incriminating evidence was pointing to. Would such intimidation lead the commission members to rule certain evidence "unreliable" and exclude it from the commission's final report?

The Kelley investigators found that there was little doubt that President Jones was, at the very least, if not part of the original planning of the assassination attempt, a major player in its cover-up. On November 26, the day after the president was buried, Jones held a meeting in the White House with the Joint Chiefs of Staff. At that meeting, he signed executive order number 273, which reaffirmed the military commitment of the U.S. to a country in the midst of civil war with communist insurgents. The enormity of this executive order comes to light when its consequences are examined.

First of all, Jones directly countermanded President Kelley's executive order, signed shortly before his attempted assassination, to withdraw the military from that conflict. On January 23, almost 10 months to the day before they would attempt to kill him, the president issued a memo instructing that "All official visits by high-ranking military and civilian personal be coordinated with…and cleared with Governor Harrisan." In effect, Kelley was not allowing his military and intelligence people to have any further involvement in the growing war. The military was outraged. They immediately, albeit cautiously, began to plan the president's assassination.

The generals quickly brought together individuals with like hatred for the Kelleys, of which there was no small number. Among those with an interest in making sure the war continued were defense contractors. Those suppliers, some of America's largest corporate entities, had CEOs who stood to make tens of millions of dollars personally by keeping the war machine supplied, the cost of which would exceed $300 Billion dollars.

During the conflict, which ensued, the United States lost over five thousand helicopters, hundreds of thousands of rifles, and hundreds of carrier-and land-based fighter jets. The country spent hundreds of millions of rounds of ammunition and dropped 6.5 million bombs. Not to mention billions of gallons of gasoline used. More than fifty-seven thousand American servicemen lost their lives to the conflict. Hundreds of thousands more were injured. At one point, over five hundred thousand U.S. servicemen were involved in the war at the same time.

Next to join the growing group of conspirators was the entire intelligence community, the DIA, CIA, and FBI. In a publicly humiliating fashion, Kelley had fired CIA Director Dunlap just 16 months prior to his assassination attempt. The Director was openly livid and publicly vocal. Why would President Jones later assign Dunlap to the Werner Commission to investigate the assassination of a president he openly hated? Coincidence? Cover-up?

Defense intelligence was run by military officers directly beholden to generals at the Pentagon. Their careers were dependent upon how they handled the "assignments" those generals gave them. These assignments were never fully explained, and were always part of larger projects the full scope of which was never revealed to individual agents. The Army chief of staff could give one agent an order to have the president's body taken to Walter Reed Army Hospital, order another to have the brain removed for "examination," and then command another to deliver the president's body to Bethesda Naval Hospital for autopsy. None of the agents involved had to know the final outcome of their actions.

The FBI director had as much hatred for the Kelleys as the others did. In the years following his appointment by Jack Kelley, Robert Kelley, as attorney general, went out of his way to belittle FBI Director Jay Howard. He cut him off from having direct access to the president, a privilege he had enjoyed while serving the four presidents in office before Kelley. Howard almost certainly knew of the assassination. The Secret Service, which operates under the FBI, was directly involved in the attempted killing. The week of the president's trip to Texas, many of his regular contingents of security people were reassigned and told to go on vacation, and were substituted with others. Was it simply coincidence that some members of the president's Secret Service detail were out drinking in Jack Sarubi's strip joint until 3:30 AM the morning of the president's visit?

Primary responsibility for advance security preparations for the president's Dallas visit was with Special Agent Phil Morrison, a member of the White House detail, and Clayton Worrels, special agent in charge of the Dallas office. The Dallas trip had been scheduled months before, but they were not officially advised of the trip until November 4. It was Morrison's responsibility, among other things, to secure the presidential motorcade route. That usually included placing sharpshooters on buildings along the route and rounding up anyone known to be a threat to the president. Osborn should have been on the top of that list.

These agents were the only ones authorized to make changes to the route the presidential motorcade was to take. The change that Morrison made, a relatively minor one, caused the limo to take a sharp left turn rather than the originally planned much softer left. This sharp left caused the president's limo to slow down, to below the speed recommended by the Secret Service, giving the assassins a better shot.

Lincoln Jones participated in a concerted effort by the FBI, CIA, and the Mafia to provide the public with misinformation about the assassination. For example, in January of that year, a Las Vegas gangster, Johnny Roselli, whose story was leaked to the press by the FBI director himself, claimed that Fidel Castro had killed President Kelley. It eventually became clear who had given him this idea. Months after Roselli made his claim about Castro, President Jones gave an interview to newsman Howard K. Smithson. During the interview President Jones dramatically asserted, "I'll tell you something that will rock you. Kelley was trying to get Castro, but Castro got him first."

Misinformation, mixing one part truth with three parts lies, was the order of the day in the months after the assassination attempt. The Werner Commission utterly disregarded compelling evidence pointing to the truth about the shooting of President Jack Kelley—with FBI files flowing between the FBI and the Jones White House anyone who dared get in the way of this was "investigated" by the FBI or the IRS and quickly fell into line, or was found dead, often under suspicious circumstances.

CHAPTER 14

▼

FOUR MORE YEARS

With the sudden and unexpected death of President Jones who had been nominated to run for President in early July at the Atlantic City Republican convention, President Kelley had a series of political mountains to climb in his bid to be reelected. His problem was not attracting voters—he fully expected to beat anyone he was up against—but rather the election laws of each state, and figuring out what he needed to do to get on each state's ballot. Weak and still recovering from his long ordeal, Kelley began by inviting congressional Republican leaders and key Republican strategists for luncheons at the White House. The Republican Party needed a standard-bearer to head the national ticket for both president and vice president.

President Kelley didn't want to run with a VP selected by Jones. He naturally wanted to run with a vice president of his own choosing, one he felt comfortable with. He would insist on having his own running mate, but if the legal problems associated with removing Jones' choice were insurmountable, or if the political fallout was too great, he would give in and go with Jones' choice. With the election less than seventy days away, party leaders needed to act fast. Kelley proposed that the leaders contact each of the delegates to the Atlantic City convention and have them sign a notarized statement nominating him for the party's choice as president and affirming Missouri governor John Cummings as his choice for running mate.

Cummings had been a successful businessman before running for public office. He served two terms in Congress before becoming governor. He was a young, energetic family man, and being from Missouri he gave a nice geographic balance to the ticket. John got along well with Jack and Bobby Kelley, and their entire staff gave him the thumbs-up.

President Kelley next had to submit legal challenges in every state in which Jones had won the primary. Most states had written into their election laws the right of the nominating party to substitute the name of a nominee in the event of the nominee's death. Most of these challenges would be academic, but they would require coordination in sending attorneys to file motions in each state capital. These attorneys would have to have significant knowledge in presenting the case in accordance with that states election laws. As if all this wasn't enough, the president also had to be concerned with campaigning. Given the lapse of security in Dallas, which nearly cost him his life, he was understandably reluctant to trust his travel to normal security people.

The president appointed his longtime friend Todd Dwyer to run his campaign. Todd was a mature southern businessman with an easy and friendly demeanor, and a perfect choice to soothe southern uneasiness over Kelley's reelection. Kelley trusted Todd to be sensitive to all the particular problems this election would produce. This election would no doubt be the most unconventional presidential election in the history of the United States.

Several weeks after President Kelley reemerged, Sean had finished his homework on all three of the assassins. The first up was Salvatore Falcone, a 45-year-old with a rap sheet as long as the average man's arm. He had been arrested fifteen times and charged with various crimes but only convicted six times. He was in and out of jail for various crimes ranging from armed robbery to assault to dealing in cocaine and heroin.

With the CIA dossier sent by Rome station chief Morgantheau in hand; Sean McDonald had a relatively easy time tracking down the comings and goings of the three Corsican shooters. His plan was to "do" one of them at a time over a one-week or ten-day period. He and his friend Special Forces Major Joe Santora would be the only ones to handle bringing the attempted assassins to justice. Santora was a good pick for this assignment. He had grown up in Jersey City and knew many of the New Jersey wise guys. He knew how these street people thought and how they might react and he spoke fluent Italian with a Rome dialect. In his early 30's he graduated from St. Peter's College in Jersey City and then joined the Marines. Santora was single, smart and streetwise.

Bobby Kelley was right, they would never be able to gather enough evidence against these killers and even if they could, Italy would never send them back to the states to face the death penalty, it was against Italian Law to do so. It would be up to Sean to be judge, jury and executioner. As Sean made his discrete inquiries about these murderers, foreign intelligence officers began to realize from their own well-connected sources that inquiries of the three were being made. They were even more nervous about the fact that the inquiries were coming out of the White House.

Salvatore Falcone was living large. He had converted all but a small amount of the heroin he was paid into cash, and was a celebrity in the criminal circles he traveled in. Nearly everyone in his close-knit circle of "friends" knew he was one of the Kelley shooters. He had a new house built for his 80-year-old mother, who now resided in the small hillside town of Cologna, with a population of about 600, Cologna was about an hour west of Florence.

Once a month Salvatore took the long trip to visit his ailing mother. He would board a twin-engine plane that would leave Naples at six in the evening and arrive in Florence at about 7:15. In Florence, Falcone would rent a car and then drive the sixty miles to Cologna. The roads were somewhat narrow, one lane each way. The last four miles were cut out of the side of the mountain. On one side the terrain went up several hundred feet, and on the other side of the road the land fell off into a very steep ravine. On the topside of the road there were plenty of trees for cover.

Sean had planned things well. He and Santora would fly from the States to a U.S. Air Force base in Germany and then into Florence on a military transport. It was not unusual for officers to request and get free transportation on regularly scheduled military flights. There were never any records kept of who traveled where, as pilots were never requested to keep passenger logs. Sean and Joe Santora could travel to Florence without leaving any record of who they were or where they went. They would carry military-issue .45 caliber side arms and a small backpack. The plane would spend the evening in Florence and return the next day, the crew refreshed and ready for the return flight.

If all went as planned, Sean and Santora would leave Washington Thursday night at about eight and arrive in Germany at ten the next morning. The two-hour flight from Germany to Florence would arrive at around noon. Then they would rent a car and travel toward Cologna, and stop one mile outside the town. There they would plant a half-pound of CO_2 plastic explosive, which would be detonated remotely. The force of the explosion would not only kill the occupants of the targeted vehicle, but would throw their car off the road and down the 250-foot embankment. The chances of surviving such a blast were nil.

According to the plan Sean and Santora had carefully devised, Sean would stay on the hill just above the bomb and wait for Falcone's rented car. Santora, would drive back to the airport, wait for Falcone, and then follow him at a distance, maintaining constant radio contact with Sean. Sean would use a remote detonator to set off the bomb, and then get in the car with Santora. They would go back to Florence, get a good meal, and sleep on the plane, ready for the return trip.

As Brigadier General McDonald and Major Santora walked into the Florence airport terminal the day of their planned attack on Falcone, three well-dressed Italian men approached them.

"Excuse me General McDonald, my name is Captain Federico Presta. I am with the Italian Ministry of Defense. May I have a moment of your time, sir?"

Stepping out of the flow of traffic and off to the side, Captain Presta continued, "General, we are aware of exactly why you have traveled to Florence." Captain Presta's English pronunciation was perfect albeit with a very slight Italian accent. "General, I would like you to know, the matter that brings you here is part of my assignment." In the past twenty-four hours I have taken care of two of your problems. Mr. Falcone is the final phase of my assignment here. There are four more targets in your country."

Sean listened and then as if to brush Captain Presta and his two men aside he motioned to Santora to move on, then said, "Captain, I have no idea what you are talking about."

As if out of nowhere, four uniformed police officers carrying .45 caliber machine guns appeared. Captain Presta, still in a conciliatory voice said, "General, will you and the major kindly follow me? I do not wish to cause an embarrassing incident, but I must insist that you follow me."

With Captain Presta and his two companions leading the way and the four uniformed police officers bringing up the rear, the general and Major Santora were escorted up one flight of stairs and into a posh room furnished with a long table. In exquisitely pronounced Italian, the captain asked to have lunch with coffee brought up for him, his two companions, and his two guests.

One of the police officers left the room to comply with his orders. Two of the police officers stood at the door, the other across the room.

"I'm sorry, General, but I must detain you for a few hours," Captain Presta apologized. "You see, General, we had planned for this eventuality from the very beginning. I will have you back on your plane in a few hours. In the meantime, is there something I can get you to help pass the next several hours?"

His anger beginning to show, Sean said, "Captain Presta, you can't just kidnap and detain a United States general. Do you know who I am?"

"I do know who you are, General, and I know why you have come to Italy. We do not want to cause an international incident, and neither of us would want to publicly explain why we are here. Please indulge me sir, and allow me to complete this portion of my assignment," the Captain said. "Exactly what is your assignment," Sean asked. "General, in a very short period of time that will become abundantly clear," Captain Presta replied.

There was little Sean could do. The Captain was right, last thing he wanted was to draw attention to why he was in Italy. The press would have a field day speculating about what the president's top-ranking security officer and his second in command were doing in Italy with plastic explosives. Sean had little choice but to go along with Captain Presta's directive.

Several hours later a knock on the door prompted Captain Presta to step outside. He was only gone a minute or two before he returned and announced, "General, you are free to go. Your plane has been refueled and your pilot and crew have been informed that you will be boarding in just a few minutes."

"You do realize, Captain," Sean said, "that we will have to return to complete our intended mission."

"I doubt that, General," Captain Presta shot back. "You see, while you and Major Santora were enjoying a quiet afternoon as my guests, my men saw to it that your mission was completed. You will shortly learn from your own sources, that there is no reason for you to return to complete your assignment. After you have had some time to think about it General, you will no doubt agree that this was the best way to handle what had to be done,"

Not wanting to acknowledge one way or the other what he was there to accomplish, Sean at first did not respond. But his curiosity got the best of him, and he had to ask, "Tell me, Captain Presta, why would the Italian Ministry of Defense want to eliminate three known contract killers? Whose orders does your Defense Ministry march to?"

Captain Presta replied, "General, it is not a question of whose orders we march to. Actually, no one has given any orders. We are acting simply in the best interest of the Italian government. We want to make sure these men are not available to create further scandal either in your country or ours. You see General, had these men been exposed and the media made aware of their involvement in the attempted assassination of your president, it would have led to a number of, let me say, embarrassing revelations."

"What kind of embarrassing revelations, Captain?"

"I am not at liberty to say, General," Presta continued. "Let's just say that we are working very closely with the national intelligence officers from a number of countries, including the United States. We have underway several very intricate undercover operations involving terrorist groups around the world. Some of these U.S. intelligence officers could be drawn into the conspiracy to kill your president, and that, General, could lead to a major breach of security in our undercover operations. We can not always chose who we work with in my line of work, I do not condone what these people have done, however, revealing their identity now would do more harm than good."

"You do realize Captain, we are at odds on this issue. We intend to deal with these conspirators," Sean said. "As do we," Presta replied, "however, I believe our method of dealing with this problem will differ from yours."

With that Captain Presta bid a warm farewell to the Americans and motioned to the police to escort the general and Major Santora to their awaiting airplane.

It was Saturday afternoon when Sean and Santora arrived back in Washington. The first thing Sean did was call Bobby Kelley to ask for a meeting as soon as possible. They agreed to meet at ten on Monday morning. Next, Sean checked his intelligence sources to confirm what he already knew would check out, that Salvatore Falcone was dead. Sure enough, he was informed, Falcone was shot to death on Friday afternoon as he hailed a cab to go to the Naples airport for his trip to Florence. Italian police were reporting the hit as a drug-related murder. The other two Corsicans had been killed in unrelated incidents. One had died in a head-on collision while driving under the influence of alcohol. The other had had a massive coronary failure while having dinner with his family. With all three shooters now dead, apparently killed to tidy up some loose ends, Sean couldn't help but wonder about the identities of the four people Captain Presta had said were targeted in his stateside mission, and about exactly who had ordered the killings.

For the first time in months, Sean spent Saturday evening having a quiet dinner with his wife. These past ten or eleven months had kept him away much of the time. They talked at length about the kids and some of the things that kept him away from home. He felt somewhat vindicated and even proud in explaining his involvement in protecting the President since the assassination.

Monday morning, rested from a Sunday spent relaxing with his family, Sean headed to the attorney general's office for his meeting with Bobby. When he arrived he was greeted by Bobby's receptionist and then escorted into Bobby's office. Bobby started the meeting by saying, "I saw some intelligence reports this morning. Apparently this drug dealer in Naples, a guy named Falcone, was shot dead hailing a cab. It's being reported as a drug hit. Nice work, Sean. That should send the bastards a message!"

"Bobby, I know you said you don't want to know the details, but you need to know something. I didn't do it."

"What do you mean you didn't do it?"

Sean went on to explain about the encounter with Captain Presta in Florence.

"So who is this Presta guy?" Bobby wanted to know. "We also need to find out who these four stateside targets are." "When I leave here," Sean said, "I'm going over to pick this guy's mug out of our files on international intelligence operatives."

Bobby directed the conversation to a different priority. "We've got two weeks until the election," he said. "I'm going to be totally wrapped up in making sure that Jack gets reelected, so let's put a lid on all your activities until after the election. Continue to gather intelligence on these insiders, but wait until after Jack is reelected to act on anything. We'll have plenty of time after the election to take our pound of flesh."

On November 4, President John F. Kelley and Vice President John Cummings were elected in a landslide victory that won them every state in the Union.

The following day Bobby called Sean, "Ok Sean, let's go ahead with our project to get to the bottom of who Captain Presta is so interested in."

About the Author

Born and raised in New Jersey, James J. Shanni married Evelyn in 1964. He had three children and moved to Atlanta, GA in 1973 to raise his family. In the 1960's he worked for United Press International (UPI) and covered the 1964 Democratic National Convention in Atlantic City, as telephoto operator and freelance photographer. Several of his pictures made front page on a number of major newspapers including the *Herald Tribune, Chicago Daily News*, etc. He has spent the past 35 years as President and CEO of his own manufacturing firm and is currently enjoying his 5 grandsons, Jake; Owen; James Patrick; Nicholas; Samuel and granddaughter Josephine and anxiously awaiting grand-child number 7.

978-0-595-67231-
0-595-67231-0